SECRETS OF THE ORCHARD

JEAN KELLY

Visit our website at www.StillwaterPress.com for more information.

First Stillwater River Publications Edition

ISBN-13: 978-1-946300-77-5
ISBN-10: 1-946300-77-2
ISBN-EBOOK: 978-0-692-11161-1

Library of Congress Control Number: 2018956405

1 2 3 4 5 6 7 8 9 10

Written by Jean Kelly
Design by Courtney Lopes

Published by Stillwater River Publications, Pawtucket, RI, USA.
Secrets of the Orchard is a work of fiction. The names, characters, places, and incidents are the product of the author's imagination or are used fictitiously. Any resemblance to actual persons, living or dead, businesses, organizations, events, is entirely coincidental.

The views and opinions expressed in this book are solely those of the author and do not necessarily reflect the views and opinions of the publisher.

This book is dedicated to families who are searching for truths from the past for answers to questions that long-ago generations never meant to be asked—and to my beloved husband Dave and my loving family for their constant encouragement and support.

PROLOGUE

Tuesday, March 8, 1955

Old Town Hospital, Springton, Massachusetts

The shuffling noise of rubber soles slapping on dull floor tile and the clattering of the medicine cart woke him, pulling him out of the dark pool of sleep that held no dreams but no nightmares either. When the sounds came closer without so much as a pause at the other rooms, Eric Von Der Hyde knew the second shift had begun and the lazy nurse was on duty. Unlike the day nurses, who started their rounds at the head station, she began her shift at the far end of the corridor.

By starting and finishing near the back stairs, across from his room, she could sneak two cigarette breaks.

The lingering smells of institutional soap over collective body odor were like foul smelling salts to his nostrils. Forcing himself fully awake, he figured out the time. *Second shift meant three p.m. Julian must be on his way.* Tasting the sweat on his lips, Eric braced for the pain that would increase at any minute. Like clockwork, it began somewhere deep within his body until it surfaced to his skin and then seeped to the top of his head and the soles of his feet.

The injection would take hold right away and plunge him into the pit of blackness, perhaps for the last time. He couldn't afford that today. He needed the minutes the nurse would take away if she medicated him now.

The nurse dragged the cart through the doorway and then moved an orange vinyl chair that separated the two beds. After setting a syringe on the bedside table, she lifted Eric's bony wrist to take his pulse. *Not yet,* he wanted to scream out but the words froze in his throat. With stiff fingers, he scratched at the coarse sheet.

"Don't get excited," she said, without looking at him. "You'll get your shot in a minute."

He tried to make his lips and tongue move together to loosen the words so they could be blown out by what was left of his breath.

His chest sank in under the sheet and when he exhaled, the command came out like an explosion. *"No!"* The effort left him with thunder in his ears and pounding in his head.

She dropped his arm, startled. "No shot then," she said quickly. "Whatever you think is best." She turned away, and it gave him satisfaction to know she was unnerved. She put the syringe back on the cart. "I forgot," she said. "You're having a visitor today. I guess it's because you're new. After a while, people don't bother to come here anymore." She looked at the still, gaunt figure in the next bed. "He can wait. I'll be back."

Eric watched her drag the cart back over the threshold and park it in the hallway. She disappeared from his view and in seconds, he heard the metal door leading to the staircase open and shut with a clang.

His shrunken stomach lurched at the thought of the cigarette smoke that would reek from her when she returned. How ironic, he thought, when it was his years of smoking that put him here in the first place. His mind drifted to the other thing that brought him here, the secret that he himself had only discovered four years earlier, one that would soon be revealed. He was sure he had made the right decision: letting the only family he had remember him the way he was before this lousy illness—and relying on his childhood friend to help him for the first time in his life.

Games, Eric thought. *Everything's a game.* Like the physical and mind games he and Julian had played when they were kids. Who could outsmart the other, who could endure the most. It never mattered what the game was. Eric always won. When they were young, Julian had depended upon Eric. Now, it was the other way around.

And he knew that if Julian didn't get here soon, it would be too late.

CHAPTER ONE

Tuesday, March 8

Julian Baker stared at the grimy door of Building C and thought, *Welcome to Old Town Hospital, where people go to die.* He covered the dirty knob with his handkerchief and opened the door.

The odor emanating from the foyer was all too familiar, the kind of smell that usually came to him only after it was reduced to a faint trace. He stepped into the foyer and stood while the stench, like a wave from a polluted ocean, washed over him, reminding him of the first time he came to this building years ago.

His father had sent him to pick up a body, the first of many. Julian had just turned sixteen, with a new driver's license, and so eager to get behind the wheel of a vehicle, any vehicle, that it didn't matter it was a hearse, or that its air conditioner was broken.

He remembered that August day. He had taken with him Wendell, who did occasional jobs at his father's funeral home. Wendell, usually somber and jittery, had laughed out loud when Julian sped along winding, secondary roads.

Later, when they'd returned to the funeral home, Julian and Wendell carried the lumpy bag to the embalming room where

Julian's father waited, an impatient, disapproving expression on his face.

His father had told Julian he had more work than he could handle, and this was the day his son would do his first embalming, whether he liked it or not.

Julian remembered very well the nausea that overcame him on that day. But most of all, he would never forget the clicking sound of the key when his father had locked the door behind him, leaving Julian alone until the job was done.

Now here he was, twenty-five years later, perspiring on this sunless, chilly March day as he had on that summer afternoon that seemed a lifetime ago. Only this time, he wasn't picking up a body. He would have Wendell do that later.

Now Julian was here to see his childhood friend Eric Von Der Hyde. He had thought the phone call for him to come out here was a joke. It was absurd to think that a career United States Army officer who had served several tours of duty would be a patient in this God-forsaken place. There were better hospitals for officers.

Julian heard quick footsteps. A young nurse, wearing a starched white uniform with a pinafore apron, approached him. "Are you Mister Julian?" she asked.

Irritated, he said, "That's my first name. I am Julian Baker."

"I'm sorry," she said. "I must have misread the notation on the chart."

"Think nothing of it," he said with a forced smile.

"I'm Nurse Hanson," she said. "My shift is over, but I'll take you to Eric. It's after three. We need to hurry before his medication takes effect."

Julian followed her down a long hallway. "Eric is terminal, I was told, when I got the phone call. Is that true?"

"Yes, larynx cancer. End stages."

So Eric had come home to die and be buried in his family's plot. He was relying on his hometown friend to handle the arrangements, expecting a favor to be returned after all these years. Eric wouldn't want his sisters to see him like this. It was that simple.

Julian tried not to smile at the possibilities.

§

It was his eyes that distinguished Eric Von Der Hyde from the man in the next bed.

Like twin coins under a magnifying glass, they reflected a silvery cast, a cast that matched the gray light piercing the window panes. The knowing stare that Julian had seen Eric use so many times on others was now fixed on him.

"I'm sorry, old friend," Julian said, touching the thin arm resting on the sheet. He quickly withdrew his hand when he saw the gray eyes narrow, giving warning. And he saw something else in Eric's eyes: a man being devoured by pain.

Julian in his wildest dreams never thought he would see the body of Eric Von Der Hyde, former star athlete, metamorphosed into this emaciated form.

Eric opened his mouth to speak, but the words didn't come. He watched Julian in appraising silence.

Julian stood, trying to meet that silver gaze, and feeling oddly nervous. The silence in the room was unbearable. If Eric couldn't communicate, he'd get the nurse he saw dawdling in the hallway to help.

Clearing his throat, Julian said, "I had dinner at Meg's last Sunday. She's a great cook, just like your mother was." He wanted to scream, *Talk, for God's sake. Don't stare at me with those eyes.* Instead, he added, "I hear Ellen is fine, too. Meg says she has a wonderful life in Boston. You must be glad your sisters are doing well."

Eric's gaze was unrelenting. *The man's body might be gone, but his mind is very much intact,* Julian thought. He continued making small talk, about how Springton hadn't changed much. Most of the people from school had moved on, and just a handful were left. Just himself, Meg and her husband Carl, and the King brothers.

"You remember them," Julian went on. "Jeremy and Bruce, always picking on me when we were kids. Well, they're police officers now. And good ones, too. You never know about people, do you?"

He knew he was talking too fast. His face felt flushed. The stale air was suffocating. Didn't they ever open the windows in this place? He tugged at his tie and loosened the collar of his shirt.

The noise of rickety wheels and rattling bottles coming closer seemed to give Eric strength. Eric moved his head ever so slightly, toward a nightstand with white peeling paint.

Julian, relieved that the eyes were no longer riveted on him, understood. He opened the top drawer and took out two envelopes.

The first was addressed to him, and he slid it open. It contained a legal, notarized document with burial instructions and a check to cover expenses.

When Julian saw the name on the second envelope, he felt the blush spread, with the speed of a brushfire, from his neck to his forehead. He wanted to curse the trait that had plagued him from childhood. His hands trembled so slightly that only someone who knew him very well would notice.

Eric's eyes locked onto his, and Julian looked to the floor, realizing he had revealed himself. After all these years, the only friend he ever had could still read him. Worse, when Julian looked again at Eric, he knew what Eric was thinking, that maybe he had made a mistake in giving Julian the papers.

Eric's face contorted with pain as he lifted his hand off the sheet. "Papers, give back," was the hissing command. Skeletal fingers reached out, scratching the top sheet.

Powerless, thought Julian. For all the awards in high school, and the Army medals, Eric was now the weakling. Julian felt stronger than he had in his life. The heat disappearing from his cheeks, he tore open the second envelope and quickly scanned the first page. It was all he needed to know for now.

"Don't get so excited," he said, putting the letter in his coat pocket. "You did the right thing in having me called."

He took Eric's hand. "I will follow your instructions and deliver the letter to Meg personally. It will give me one more reason to see her." Julian couldn't help grinning. "Thank you, my friend."

Gurgling noises of protest came from Eric's mouth. Julian deliberately tightened the pressure of the handshake.

Eric didn't flinch, and Julian had to marvel at this last show of strength. But when Eric's eyes changed from high polished silver to battleship gray, Julian knew he was being warned. It unnerved him. But he didn't know why. After all, dead men can't talk.

And Julian knew, simply by looking at him, that Eric was almost dead.

CHAPTER TWO

Tuesday, March 8

Boston, Massachusetts

A gust of March wind from Boston Harbor caught the brim of the slender woman's hat just as she stepped off the streetcar. Holding the hat down with one hand and keeping her flared skirt in place with the other, her shoulder bag slipping to her elbow, she crossed the wide avenue to a one-family brick house on the corner. A hand-printed Studio Apartment for Rent sign was posted in the front window. She pushed the bag up to her shoulder, hurried up the steps, and pressed the doorbell.

A stout, middle-aged woman opened the door. "You must be Ellen Von Der Hyde," she said, her pleasant voice rich with a Polish accent. "I remember our conversation because you were the only female who called about the apartment."

"Yes, I am," said Ellen. "And you are Mrs. Nowak?"

"Yes, come in. The wind is kicking up more."

Ellen stepped into the foyer, her eyes going straight to the winding, wooden staircase with its well-polished bannister. Old gas lamps converted to small electric bulbs cast an amber glow that cut through the stream of gray light filtering through the windows.

The woman looked at Ellen from head to toe, taking in the hat that tilted to the side of her long auburn hair, gray wool jacket with a belt cinched at the waist, white blouse tied at the neck with a neat bow, plaid skirt, and low-heeled pumps.

Mrs. Nowak gestured at a coat stand near the door, and Ellen removed her hat and jacket. As she smoothed out the shoulder pads of her blouse, she felt a run in her nylons inching along her left leg. *Well, now it will match the one on the right*, she thought wryly.

"You said you have references?"

"Oh, yes," Ellen said, reaching into her bag and taking out a folded letter. "I'm a boarder at Lynhaven, a residence for women."

Scanning the letter, Mrs. Nowak said, "And you said you work for a newspaper?"

"Yes, I'm a feature writer with the *Daily Call*. I've worked there for six months now."

Mrs. Nowak pointed to the open, winding staircase. "As you know, the apartment is on the third floor, and it is completely furnished, even with dishes. I think there are only one or two pans, though."

"I'm not much of a cook, Mrs. Nowak. One or two pans is plenty."

The woman continued to talk as she led Ellen up the stairs. "I had to make the top floor into an apartment after my husband was killed in the war. He loved this country so much, he would have been proud knowing he died serving it."

"I'm very sorry," said Ellen as they reached the top landing. "My brother, Eric, has been in the army for a very long time. He's in Germany right now, but next year he's retiring and moving back to our hometown."

"Ah, God willing," said Mrs. Nowak, opening the door to the apartment.

Ellen was completely taken with the furnishings. The appliances were vintage 1930s: a gas stove on four legs with a match tin on its shelf; a coffee percolator on the back burner, and a toaster on a Formica table. A pullout couch was ideally situated near the bay windows and next to it a small desk, just right for her upright typewriter, one of her few possessions.

"This is perfect," said Ellen, "but when we talked I couldn't hear what the rent was. There was interference on the phone."

Shaking her head, Mrs. Nowak said, "Party telephone lines. Nosy people listening in. The rent is two-hundred-and-fifty dollars a month."

Disappointment in her voice, Ellen said, "I can't afford that right now."

"But you have a good job," said Mrs. Nowak.

Ellen smiled. After all these years, she could finally talk about it, and she liked Mrs. Nowak's directness. "Yes, I have a good job, but I had a bad marriage. I was a small-town girl who moved to Boston to go to college, but I went and fell in love with another student, and we ran off and got married."

"So this man was no good?"

Ellen's smile disappeared. In a soft voice, she said, "I soon learned he was a gambler, and I left him. But he put us so much in debt that I had to drop out of full-time college. I finally graduated after years of night courses. I'm still paying off his debts." She paused, taking a long look at the apartment she couldn't have. Forcing a smile, she said, "But, in six months, I'll be able to afford a beautiful apartment, just like this one."

Mrs. Nowak's eyes narrowed. "This man. Did you go after him for what he owed you?"

"No. He covered his tracks pretty well. Besides, the money I would have paid a detective was better spent on the divorce, which I got, along with my maiden name. That was very important to me. Getting back my identity."

When they returned to the foyer, Mrs. Nowak opened a door

to the left of the stairs. "Please step inside to my home," she said. "If you have time, that is."

Glancing at the slim wristwatch that was once her mother's, Ellen said, "My boss, Wayne Ellis—he's the head of the features department—said I could take the morning off, but I really should go and look at other apartments."

"This will just take moments," said Mrs. Nowak. "Please."

Mrs. Nowak gestured to a table where a man in his thirties and a boy about nine were looking at the pages of an open book. "This is my nephew Marek and his son Stefan," Mrs. Nowak said.

Marek looked up, nodded at Ellen, and went back to the book, pointing to a sentence. "Try to read it again," he said to the boy.

Mrs. Nowak sighed. "Marek brought his wife and son over to help me with this property. But Stefan is having such problems at school that the teacher wants to hold him back. The boy has trouble learning to read in English. Maybe you can help him and in return we can do something about the rent?"

Hesitating at first, Ellen said, "I'm not a teacher, but I read to my little niece and nephew when I visit them ... so yes, maybe I could help Stefan." She noticed that Stefan shrank away from the table when she spoke.

"See? That teacher has made him afraid." Mrs. Nowak gestured for Ellen to sit.

Ellen reached for a children's book on the table. The title was in Polish, with animals and birds on the cover. "Stefan, may I read this book?" she asked. When he nodded, Ellen began to read, struggling to pronounce the words. Stefan's serious expression turned into a smile, and he giggled.

"Be polite," scolded his father.

"Stefan," Ellen said softly. "Will you help me learn how to read this book and I will help you with English?"

"Yes, yes," said the boy.

Mrs. Nowak and Marek exchanged glances, then Mrs. Nowak spoke rapidly in Polish to Marek.

"Yes, Aunt," said Marek. "I am completely in agreement."

Mrs. Nowak, turning to Ellen, said, "Two hundred dollars a month for six months. Is that acceptable to you?"

"Oh yes," said Ellen, already out of her chair. "I'll be right back with my things. It won't take long, believe me."

CHAPTER THREE

Wednesday, March 9

Ellen woke up at five a.m., her mind on the biggest news tip that had ever came her way. If she wasn't at her desk at seven, the informant who called himself Jake said he'd hang up if anyone else answered. And she knew he meant it.

The temperature of the studio apartment was cool but bearable. Ellen pulled on a bulky sweater over her flannel pajamas and took the few steps to the kitchenette. She measured coffee from a metal tin, poured water into the well-worn percolator, and lit the front burner with a long kitchen match.

While the coffee brewed, she ran the hot water spigot in the claw-footed tub in the bath just off the kitchenette, her mind on Jake's tip. He had said there was a counterfeiting ring operating right in the middle of the city. If it checked out, she would have her first hard news story. She let her thoughts run along with the running water. *Maybe there's a new career ahead for me. From feature writer to star investigative reporter.* She dipped her hand in the water, then sighed. The tub water was barely lukewarm.

First lesson, she thought. *Run the hot water before preparing the coffee.* Tomorrow morning there would be time to luxuriate in the deep tub.

When the hot water pipes on the walls finally shook and cranked, Ellen was washed and dressed, wearing a white pullover sweater topped with a navy blue boxer jacket and a matching pencil skirt. Looking over her shoulder at the antique, long mirror which tilted on its wooden stand, she awkwardly checked the backs of her legs to make sure the seams of her nylons were straight. "I don't know which I hate more, the stockings or the garter belt holding them up," she muttered.

At the door, she pulled a white winter wool hat down over her ears. Then she looked at a small table where she had arranged three photos, the first of her belongings she had unpacked.

The black-and-white photos were set in German silver frames, gifts from her brother, Eric. She touched the center photo of her stoic-looking parents, Esther and Rudolph, the familiar wave of sadness sweeping over her at the thought of their fatal car accident four years earlier. She quickly turned her glance to the photo on her right. The radiant smiles of her sister, Meg, and her family seemed to beam through the picture glass, making Ellen break out into a smile of her own.

To the left of her parents' photo was the picture of Eric, so handsome in his Army uniform, a thin smile on his lips. On an impulse, which she didn't think about until much later, she reached for his photo and stared at his gray eyes, their intensity captured in black and white, eyes that were so similar to her own. "In just a year, you'll be home," she whispered. "We'll be a family again."

She gently put Eric's photo back in its place, then set her mind on the day ahead. And the phone call that depended on a snitch keeping his word.

CHAPTER FOUR

Her desk phone jangled on the dot of seven. "Ellen Von Der Hyde," she said, crisply, trying to keep the anxiety from her voice. A gravelly voice crackled through the phone wire. "I'm only callin' ya' this once, lady. I'm leavin' on the next train."

"Hello, Jake," Ellen said, loud enough to signal her co-worker, Nick Stanton, to listen in from the phone on his desk across from hers. "You're calling from a phone booth at South Station?"

"Yeah. And I ain't puttin' another nickel in."

"Let's get right to it," she said, cradling the receiver between her shoulder and chin and then picking up a pencil with her right hand. "The counterfeiting ring. Do you know where the money is made?"

"Yeah. In the cellar of a pawnshop."

She rolled her eyes at Nick, who held his phone receiver to his ear. "There are a lot of pawnshops, Jake. Which one?"

"Hold your horses, lady. I need to light up." The strike of a match grated across the telephone line. "Carbury Street, across from the Star Luncheonette." He inhaled deeply, then said, "I wouldn't be able to stand up here if it wasn't for you saving me.

My legs would have been crushed. Or worse. I might even be dead."

Nick caught her eye and waved for her to speed things up. She shook her head. There was no rushing this weary, ill man, who seemed to be trying to stay a step ahead of people who were after him. Ellen shivered at the memory of the small, fragile-looking man who had tripped and fallen under the wheels of a streetcar. He was almost bird-like, just light enough for her to grab his jacket collar and pull him away from the trolley tracks seconds before the wheels of the streetcar began to move.

They had sat on a bench and when he had stopped shaking, he noticed Ellen's name badge. "So, of all things, a reporter saved poor old Jake's life," he'd said, getting to his feet. "Lady, life is all about paybacks, and there's word on the street about a counter-feiting ring. Be at your desk day after tomorrow, seven a.m. sharp, and I'll have a tip for you."

Jake had disappeared into the crowd, and Ellen had immedi-ately checked with Marc Donovan, the *Daily Call's* new publisher, whose eyes had lit with recognition. "I'll be darned," he'd said. "That's Jake the jockey. Years ago, he was caught fixing the races and managed to cut a deal. Take his tip, Ellen. It's your story but bring Nick in on it."

Now, Ellen watched the wall clock tick away precious seconds. Aware of Nick's impatient look, Ellen pressed, "Jake, who's running this ring?"

"That's your job," he said, going into a hacking cough. "I ain't askin' no more questions on the street. You got that, lady?"

"Do you have anything else?"

In between wheezes, he said, "Yeah. There's a code. Say you want to buy a briefcase. They'll ask brown or green leather, so you say alligator green. They'll give you the case and an envelope. With fifty bucks for you and an address for you to deliver. Only you're gonna' take it right to the police station. And you get your exclusive. So, we're even."

The operator cut in. "Your three minutes are up. Insert five cents, please."

Ellen scribbled on her pad furiously. "Don't hang up, Jake."

"Make sure somebody's got your back, lady. Just like you had mine." The phone went dead.

Nick set his phone receiver on the cradle. "I don't like his warning to you."

Ellen looked up from her notes and stared at her co-worker, as if seeing him for the first time that morning. Nick's shirt was rumpled, with the sleeves rolled up to the elbows. The brown-and-red-striped tie that hung loosely around his shirt collar closely matched his deep brown eyes that were now bloodshot. Stacks of yellowed newspapers tilted on the floor. Paper coffee cups were piled around his typewriter. "You didn't go home last night, did you?"

Nick stretched and rubbed the top of his head with both hands, messing up the neatly combed side part in his light brown hair. "Very good, detective. Quite the investigator, you are. I researched old articles about counterfeiting rings that used to operate around here."

He pulled a sheet of paper out of his typewriter, attached it with a paper clip to a few pages, and walked over to Ellen. "I wrote a side story," he said, setting the pages in front of her. "It's about counterfeiting crimes in this city dating back to nineteen thirty."

She read it quickly. "This is good work. Even if Jake's tip doesn't pan out, I'm sure Marc will want to print this on the Back Then page."

"So, your guy Jake is leaving town. And only this newspaper, thanks to your heroic deed, has this tip."

"Very good, detective. Now who's the investigator?" Ellen smiled, picking up her notepad. "Let's go talk to our boss, partner. We've got a case to crack."

❧

Marc Donovan scanned Ellen's notes and quickly dialed the city detective division. "This tip is real, Ellen," he said. "Jake wouldn't waste his time if it wasn't." When a voice at the other end of the line answered, he put his hand over the mouthpiece and raised his eyebrows at Nick and Ellen. "Get back to your desks," he said, waving them away.

"Geez," Nick grumbled, back in their office. "You don't think he's going to turn all our work over to one of his investigative reporters, do you?"

"I hope not," Ellen said. "I'm ready to try my hand at the big time."

Ten minutes later, Marc came into their office, the first time Ellen could remember him taking the elevator up to their floor.

"The police will have a sting operation going down at noon." He dropped a sheet of paper, where he'd scrawled nearly illegible notes, on Ellen's desk. "The details are all there."

"It's a raid," Ellen said, excited. "Am I a part of it?"

"It's too dangerous, Ellen," Nick said at once. "I'll go in your place."

Marc held up his hand. "Slow down, you two. We're dealing with thugs. I don't need my staff ending up in the morgue. I'll work something out so you can watch the action, but absolutely no more than that."

Walking out the door, he turned and added, "And I mean it."

CHAPTER FIVE

From a booth in the front window of the Star Luncheonette, Ellen and Nick kept a watchful eye on the pawnshop across the street. Nick took the last bite of a cheeseburger while Ellen picked at a plate of French fries. She hadn't eaten anything for breakfast but had no appetite for lunch.

From a nearby church steeple, twelve bells chimed. "That's the cue," said Nick. He nodded toward a man dressed in shabby clothes who was entering the pawnshop. "He's the undercover detective. Boy, I wish we were closer."

Ellen noticed another man in the doorway of a building on the corner. He was wearing a loose-fitting trench coat over a suit. "That's got to be his partner," she whispered.

Minutes later the detective walked out of the pawnshop, carrying a green briefcase. He turned to his right, still in view of Ellen and Nick, and handed the briefcase to the man in the doorway. The man wedged open the latch on the briefcase, looked at the contents, and nodded to his partner, who spoke into a hand-held radio.

"It must be filled with money," Ellen whispered just as police officers, their badges glistening in the noon sun, began to move in from the street corners. They rushed into the pawnshop, their guns drawn. A police van sped up, then screeched to a halt in front of the luncheonette. Moments later, four men, each flanked by a pair of officers, were escorted out of the pawnshop, their cuffed hands in front of them.

Flashbulbs suddenly glared in the men's faces. Ellen gasped. *Don't tell me another newspaper is onto this*, she thought. But to her surprise, it was Nigel Jackson, their paper's top photographer, smoothly clicking one photo after another.

Irritation in her voice, Ellen said, "Nigel should be shooting from a distance. Marc didn't want any of us that close. What do you think is going on?"

Nick shrugged. "Who knows? Nigel doesn't mind taking chances. He's been doing this awhile and knows how to position himself. Or maybe Marc changed his mind and let him go in. You know how unpredictable our boss can be."

The police put the men in the back of a van. The last man was heavyset, with short-cropped hair and a square jaw set on a thick neck. He glanced around and raised his cuffed hands over his head, a sneering smile on his face. He looked vaguely familiar to Ellen, but she couldn't place him.

Nick was standing and shrugging on his jacket. "Let's go," he said, reaching into his pocket and dropping some dimes under his cup and saucer. Grinning, he lowered his voice. "You got that, lady?"

"Very funny," Ellen said, sliding out of the booth. "See if I let you listen in on any more of my tips."

᠅

Hours later, paperboys with heavy canvas bags slung over their shoulders waved newspapers from street corners. "Extra, extra, read all about it!" they shouted. In bold print, the front-page headline read: *Counterfeiting Ring Busted*, with Ellen's byline in prominent typeface. Nick's story ran on page three. Ellen had to admit Nigel's photos were remarkable. One photo, especially, stood out. Nigel had captured the menacing look on one of the counterfeiters, a man named Marty Smith, the man with the short-cropped hair. The papers were selling like hotcakes.

But Ellen didn't feel any kind of a thrill at her first front page byline. Not even later, when she stood beside Nick in the newsroom while their fellow reporters congratulated them. She remembered Jake's dire warning and Marty Smith's menacing look.

She couldn't wait to get back to writing feature stories. She'd had enough of detective work.

CHAPTER SIX

Thursday, March 10

Ellen turned off the burner and poured a cup of steaming hot coffee without adding cream and sugar. It was the second morning she had awakened in her new apartment, but it seemed as if she had barely moved in. Most of her possessions were still in hastily packed boxes, and she wasn't sure of where half her things were. The only thing she was sure about was that there would be no long, luxurious bath for her today. After Marc Donovan's startling phone call the night before, she had hardly slept at all.

Marc had called when she had returned to her apartment after tutoring Stefan. She had just put a bowl of hot chicken soup—which Mrs. Nowak had insisted she take upstairs—on the dinette table. Marc, in his usual blunt manner, had said, "Ellen, I've promoted Wayne Ellis to city page editor. I want you to take his place and head up the features department."

Ellen had blurted out the first words that came to her. "But that would make me Nick's boss. What will he think when you tell him you offered me this promotion?"

Annoyance in his voice, Marc had said, "I talked to Nick late today. It doesn't bother him at all to work for the person who got the higher position." Ellen suspected he had stopped short of saying, "and who is a female."

Incredulous that Nick was told before her, she'd decided it was best not to say that. She needed the job.

"I need a department head. That's you," he had said, before hanging up. She didn't know how long she had stood there, the dial tone buzzing in her ear.

Now here she was, again apprehensive about the day ahead of her. "Well, first things first," she said out loud, putting the coffee cup down. "Make a sandwich for your lunch."

She slapped slices of American cheese between two pieces of bread and wrapped the sandwich in waxed paper, all the while wondering if Marc was aware that she and Nick had developed an after-hours friendship. Hired on the same day, they had run into each other at the corner coffee shop and from there slid into an easy work relationship.

Ellen stuffed the sandwich into her bag, poured herself a second cup of coffee, and thought about a conversation she and Nick had a few weeks ago.

They had been sitting in what had become their favorite booth at the coffee shop, speculating on whether Marc would give out Christmas bonuses, when Nick had said, quite suddenly, "Ellen, how about if we learn a few things about each other? Strictly an edited version. Fifty words or less."

"Sure," she'd said, intrigued by the idea.

"Great, you go first."

"Fine," she'd said, then wondered what Nick might want to know. One thing she had noticed about his stories was that he had a gift for getting the people he interviewed to reveal more than they may have intended. She'd waited as the waitress set down two cups of coffee, then began. "I grew up in Springton, a small town an hour from here, worked my way through college." Her voice suddenly cracking, she added, "Both parents died in a car accident four years ago."

Nick drew in a sharp breath. "I'm very sorry," he'd said.

Clearing her throat, she continued. "My younger sister and her family live in Springton, and my older brother, who's a career Army officer, is retiring next year."

The thought of Eric returning to their hometown had made her smile. "So," she'd said, "that's about it."

Nick had taken a spoon and stirred cream into his coffee, watching the swirls dissolve.

Ellen had leaned in. "Don't try to get out of telling your life story. This was your idea."

Looking up, he'd asked softly, "Romance?"

Without hesitating, Ellen had said, "Bad marriage, quick divorce. *That's the second time this week I've been able to say those words,* she'd realized. *The past is finally behind me.* She looked at her watch. "Now your turn. Go."

Grinning, Nick said, "Raised here in Boston, only child, a very lonely one at that. I made up imaginary characters to be my friends and later wrote a children's book about them. My father died when I was five. Mother, as we speak, is sailing somewhere in the Caribbean with her third husband."

He'd paused, then smiled. "Well, since you obviously have no interest in asking me about romance, I'll volunteer it anyway. Always single, haven't dated since I took this job, and tired of people trying to fix me up." His next words took her by surprise. "We have more in common than our jobs, Ellen. Neither of us has any ties."

All she could think to say was, "That was more than fifty words."

❧

And now here she was, getting ready for work, thinking that this promotion might ruin the friendship that had been growing between her and Nick. Ellen put her coffee cup in the sink and headed for the door of her apartment. When she looked at the three photos of her family, a nagging feeling pulled at her. She had no idea what it could be, so she decided to ignore it.

For now, she needed to think about her new job.

CHAPTER SEVEN

Out on the avenue, a stiff wind was blowing, sending bits of paper and gravel swirling. Ellen kept her head down as she made her way to work.

A sound like an owl screeching stopped her in her tracks in front of the *Daily Call* building. On the curb stood a stooped woman, her hand outstretched.

"Some small change, dearie, for a bowl of hot soup," the old woman crowed. With a bony hand, she reached out and tugged at Ellen's coat sleeve. "Now, that isn't too much to ask for, is it?"

Instinctively, Ellen reached into her bag and took out the sandwich she had packed. "I'm so sorry you're hungry," she said, pressing it into the woman's hand. "Take this, please."

Ellen sidestepped the woman, wondering if there were more homeless women than men living on the city streets. It was post wartime. Many servicemen, like Mrs. Nowak's husband, had died, or, like Eric, had stayed on in the military. Maybe some of these poor women were ill, or victims of circumstances, such as a bad marriage, which she certainly understood.

Marc Donovan had insisted there were street stories, right under their noses, ready to be written. Ellen decided she would schedule an article, possibly a series, about women on the street, with photos capturing the despair on their faces. That this woman had to beg for money for food seemed an absolute outrage.

A high-pitched scream stopped Ellen in her tracks. She turned just in time to see her lunch being thrown into the gutter. The woman ran up behind her and shook her fist, screaming obscenities. Pedestrians kept their distance, going out of their way to avoid Ellen and the screaming woman. A few looked at her in annoyance, as if she should have known better.

The wind blowing at her back, Ellen stood, self-conscious and embarrassed. A reminder that she had a long way to go before she could claim to fit into city life.

A touch on her elbow startled her. It was Nick Stanton, grinning. "Hey, don't look so sad," he said, looping his arm through hers. He guided her to the entrance of the *Call's* ten-story building. "I'll retrieve your lunch, but only if you tell me it's roast beef on rye. With mustard, of course."

"It's plain cheese," Ellen said miserably.

"Well, no wonder she threw it away," Nick said. When she didn't return his smile, he said, "Look, these unfortunate things happen."

Ellen shook her arm free. "It was just a silly thing." Actually, she was thinking it would never do to be seen with Nick touching her. She thought she had reasoned things out this morning, but now, seeing Nick face to face, she had a sick feeling in the pit of her stomach. She was actually his boss now.

"Nick," she said when they stepped into the elevator. "We need to talk. My promotion is a major change. It's too much, too fast."

"Hey, if it doesn't bother me, it shouldn't bother you," he said. "But I will admit, I'll miss working in the same office with you."

"Whatever do you mean?"

Nick laughed. "Another example of Marc's impulsive nature.

He didn't mention that they moved you into the vacant office at the end of the hall? The one with the grand view of the city of Boston, two doors away from ours." His face turning serious, he caught himself. "I mean, the office we used to share."

"Oh," Ellen said, trying not to sound as startled as she felt.

The elevator came to a stop on the third floor, and she fought back a pang at the idea that they no longer shared the same space.

Walking briskly to her new office, she said, "Here's an idea for a feature story. I've heard there's a science fair at one of the high schools, and there are some great student projects. There's a model rocket engine and ideas to save energy. Find out which school, and you can write an article about the young inventors of the future."

"Oh, come on. After that counterfeiting story, that's too soft."

She turned her head slightly, but not enough for him to see her smile when she said, "So maybe you'd rather work downstairs in the newsroom instead of features?"

"Is that what you really think, Ellen?" he asked in a quiet voice.

At his serious tone, she stopped and turned. "Nick, I was joking. I guess I don't have the talent for one-liners." *And this all feels so awkward,* she added silently.

His face softened. "Let's go out to lunch today. How about some Boston clam chowder?" Then, with the mischievous grin she had grown to like so much, he added, "Seeing as I didn't retrieve your bag lunch, I should pay."

"Nick, of all days, I can't leave. I have to get organized. I need to figure out what this new job involves."

Nick shook his head and headed to his office, half the size of her new one, the office that they had shared only the day before. She had loved the clutter and the air of energy. Their combined energy. She glanced back to watch his long, lean figure take the distance in just a few strides.

Ellen had just about convinced herself that her friendship

with Nick wouldn't interfere with their work. *But now I'm begin-ning to wonder*, she thought, as she crossed the threshold, all alone, into her new office.

She settled herself at the oversized desk and started going through a file of notes that Wayne Ellis had left for her. She had barely skimmed the second page—something about a budget presentation for the department—when the phone rang. With a sigh, she leaned across the glass desktop and picked up the receiver.

She recognized the soft, halting voice immediately. It was her sister, Meg. "Ellen, I don't know how to tell you why I'm calling. It is so terrible."

"Meg, what's wrong? Is it Carl? Or the children?"

"No, no. It's Eric. He died early this morning."

Ellen turned the swivel chair to face the wall-sized window and looked down at the city sidewalks filled with people. She thought she could see her crumpled lunch bag in the gutter. "Eric?" she finally asked. "Our brother?"

"Yes. Julian just told me. I don't know what to say. Or think."

Ellen tightened her grip on the phone, as if the device could possibly give her balance. She felt suddenly detached from the call and miles away from the people rushing around on the streets. A pigeon swooped down on what might be her lunch bag, then flew away.

Even the pigeon doesn't want it, she thought. *Good grief, what am I thinking of? Anything to block out Meg's words.*

"This must be a shock to you," Meg went on. "I never really knew Eric like you did. But I feel such heartache."

Ellen nervously curled the telephone cord with her finger. "But he's only forty-one, Meg. Was it an accident?" Her mind raced. Eric was sixteen when he left home for military prep school. Ellen had been eight. They had exchanged a few letters through his first year in the army, and then he was deployed and the letters stopped. She had seen him only once after that, when their parents died in that tragic car crash four years earlier, and he had come home for the funeral.

Since then, other than Christmas gifts and an occasional post-card, there was never a word from Eric.

Speaking in a low, pained voice, Meg said, "It wasn't an accident. Eric died of cancer, right here, in the Old Town Hospital."

"Well, then it must be a case of mistaken identity. Eric's in Germany."

"No mistake. Julian saw Eric yesterday, in the hospital, just hours before he died."

"Julian?" Yes, Meg had said the news had come from Julian. The phone was pressed so hard to the side of Ellen's head that her clip-on earring dropped to the floor. "Why was Julian there and not us?" she asked tersely.

"That's exactly what I asked, but Julian's explanation makes sense. Eric was trying to spare us, that's all. He was diagnosed with a fast-moving cancer, and he wanted to come home to die and be buried in the family plot, so he requested a transfer to the hospital right here." Taking a breath, Meg added, "Julian also said the place is abominable and should be closed down."

"And what else did Julian have to say?" asked Ellen, an edge to her voice.

"Just that Eric gave him an envelope with specific burial instructions."

Ellen's voice rose. "One envelope? Our brother's entire affairs are contained in one envelope? Is that it?"

A defensive tone to her voice, Meg said, "I'm sure Julian will do whatever Eric specified in the letter. I think we're lucky to have him."

"And since he's in the funeral business, of course he'll be handling the arrangements," Ellen replied, her tone more sarcastic than she intended.

"Yes, and this will be difficult for you. The funeral's tomorrow

morning, at ten. Just a graveside service. No calling hours, nothing
in the paper."

Ellen couldn't hide her outrage. "Meg, are you telling me that
Eric wrote out his last wishes to Julian? And not us?"

"I have the letter right here. Eric's handwriting is very shaky,
but clear enough for me to read to you. Oh, this is so sad."

Ellen's thought about the last few days. So many good things
had been happening for her while her own brother lay dying only
a short distance away. She kept her tight grip on the telephone,
hanging on as if it were her lifeline, the connection to the only
family she had.

Sounding as if she were on the brink of tears, Meg read:

"'I, Eric Von Der Hyde, of sound mind, give authority to Julian Baker
to handle arrangements for my burial. I ask my family, Ellen Von Der
Hyde and Meg Anderson, to understand that I cannot communicate with
them as I had intended because the cancer that destroyed my body has now
taken away my voice. I do not want Ellen and Meg to remember me this
way. Therefore, I entrust Julian, my childhood friend, to follow my
instructions that I be buried in the Von Der Hyde plot at the Springton
Cemetery, and that he give Meg the letter.'"

Ellen interrupted. "What letter?"

Meg said, "It must be this, what I'm reading. Let me finish.
Eric ends with, 'I want a very private graveside service to take place
within twenty-four hours of my death, with no public announcement.
Enclosed is a check in the amount of five hundred dollars for expenses.'"

Meg cleared her throat. "Then there's Eric's signature and two
others who were witnesses. One is Calvin Gordon, a notary
public. The other is Sarah Hanson, RN. It's dated March 5, 1955."

"That was five days ago," Ellen said, her mind trying to make
sense of Eric's words. "What you just read sounds like a directive,
not a letter. Did Julian say anything about another letter?"

"No. We have to remember that Eric was very ill. He may
have gotten confused."

But he was of sound mind, thought Ellen. A tapping sound made her look up. Nick opened the door and pointed to his watch, reminding her of a meeting with Marc Donovan. She had so much to do. After the meeting she would need to bring Nick up to date, get back to the apartment to pack, and catch a train. There would be enough time to think about Eric's instructions when she got to Springton.

With resignation in her voice, Ellen said, "I need to talk to my boss. But I'll take the early local from South Station. I'm sorry I was so testy."

"It's okay. This is much harder on you, having to travel back here and all. I'll pick you up at the station and of course, you'll stay with us. Oh, poor Eric, coming home to die. All alone."

But it was his choice, Ellen thought. *Eric had to know what he was doing.* She remembered a line from a letter he'd sent her when he first joined the Army. It was about how he'd found a system that made sense to him. *Military precision. Everything has a strategy and no strategy is planned without a reason.*

CHAPTER EIGHT

Thursday, March 10

Springton, Massachusetts

The old monastery on the outskirts of town was set back from the road, accessible to vehicles only through wrought iron gates which opened to a dirt path cutting through a peach orchard, whose bounty had provided a living for the monks for decades. After the Hurricane of '38 destroyed the orchard, the stone building was converted to a home for the aged. Some members of the board of directors wanted to name the home The Orchard. Others had suggestions for Latin names that might be a tribute to the building's monastic history. The board members eventually compromised, with the home being named The Pomarium, the Latin translation for orchard.

Inside, a woman who had worked in the kitchen since the time before the building was converted, scraped the last of a pile of carrots, wielding her paring knife as skillfully as a barber with a razor. She put down the carrot alongside neat rows of the ones already peeled, and with a chef's knife, made swift cutting motions, then carefully slid the orange disks into a pot of boiling water.

She hardly ever looked out the back window, with its stained glass dulled by time. The beauty of the orchard had faded away, along with the memories.

The knock on the door didn't startle her because it could only be Wendell this early in the morning, with an order of eggs. Wendell worked part-time at the funeral home in town and ran deliveries for local businesses. Just to be sure, she rubbed a circle on the steamy windowpane. Then, seeing his familiar figure, she turned the handle of the aged, creaky door.

Wendell came in and set the crate on the floor. "Ten dozen, just for you, Miss Theresa," he said, taking off his cap. "There's more if you like."

Shaking her head, she selected a carton, opened it gently, and inspected each of the speckled eggs. She held the carton to her nose, nodded approval for its freshness, and then put it on a well-worn oak table in the center of the kitchen.

Wendell stood awkwardly, twisting his cap. "Miss Theresa, there's news you might want to know." He spoke in a whisper, although there was no one else around.

She turned, holding an egg she was about to crack into a porcelain bowl that contained milk and sugar for the weekly serving of custard.

"An extra job came up for me yesterday," he began. "Mr. Baker asked me to drive a hearse out to the Old Town Hospital, said he didn't want his regular drivers to know all his business. He paid me real good and told me not to tell anybody, but I never swore to it, so don't you say nothin' either."

He looked out the window and then, satisfied that no one was coming, whispered, "I picked up a body, someone you used to know from here, a long time ago." Wendell waited for her reaction, but Theresa just cracked one egg after another into the bowl, as if she wasn't listening.

Just as she took the last egg from the carton, he said, "The Von Der Hyde boy. Dead as a stone." He nodded toward the back window. "Just like the stones he used to build those monastery walls out there."

The egg dropped from her hand to the floor, its shell cracking in half. The woman stared as the bright yellow yoke slid across the crooked floorboards. A pain began in her abdomen and streaked upward toward her heart, then spread to her throat. "Are you ... sure?"

Wendell was pleased to have her attention. "I didn't believe it myself, 'cause the body weighed hardly nothin'," he said, his words coming faster. "Eric Von Der Hyde was the muscular type, built like a bull. Why, that boy could've carried four of these crates, all at once." He leaned closer to her. "It was him, all right. While Mr. Baker was in his office getting my money, I looked real close. Those eyes, they were like polished steel, looking straight out at nothin'. His mouth was open a little, like he was trying to say somethin'. I tell you, it was Eric Von Der Hyde."

She felt the pain in her throat slip downward, across her breastbone, but she forced herself to move. She pulled paper toweling from a rack, then knelt to mop up the egg, which had glided to a stop at the threshold. Without looking up, she said, "When is the funeral?"

"That's the strangest part," Wendell said, putting his cap on. "The whole thing is so private that no one is to know. It's not even to go in the papers." He waited while she cleaned up the mess so he could pass through the door. Then he said, "The funeral is tomorrow at ten. Just a graveside thing. Can you figure it out?"

Wendell hadn't been too curious when Theresa had asked him to come back in an hour and give her a ride into town. He wondered, though, what was in the big burlap bag. She refused his offer to carry it. Maybe she was afraid he would drop it, the way he had dropped a bushel of tomatoes once.

She never got upset, though, just like when she dropped the egg—just cleaned it all up, like it was nothin'.

He watched her until she was out of sight. A windy March day, but it wasn't that cold and she was wearing a heavy coat over one of those long dark dresses she wore in the kitchen. It was none of his business, he told himself, when she told him not to wait for her. Besides, he had asked her to go to the picture show with him once, and she just acted like she didn't hear him.

So let her take the bus back.

CHAPTER NINE

Friday, March 11

Springton, Massachusetts

Ellen stared at the flag-draped wooden casket set on straps above the open grave. She still couldn't believe that it was Eric in there. When the hearse had arrived at the cemetery, she had asked Julian to open the coffin, to let her see her brother for the last time. But Meg had pulled her away, saying, "No. Eric's letter said he didn't want us to remember him this way. We've got to honor his wishes."

Ellen had acquiesced, but the whole thing felt wrong to her. It was just her and Meg and Julian and the cemetery workers at the grave. Meg's little boy, Matthew, had woken up that morning with a sore throat, so Meg's husband, Carl, had stayed home with the two children. Ellen's family had never been religious, so she supposed it was fine that there was no clergyman to say prayers over the casket. But to bury Eric without anyone saying anything about his life bothered her.

Julian nodded at the cemetery workers, the signal to lower the casket.

"Wait!" Meg cried. "I just want to say that ... Eric, I never got a chance to know you very well. I wish I had. But I know you cared about us. And I hope you knew we cared about you." She stopped then, swallowing back tears.

Ellen put an arm around her sister's shoulders, keeping her gaze on the casket. "Eric, I was so looking forward to you coming home next year," she added softly. "To finally getting time to spend with my older brother. It's not fair that we never even got a chance to say good-bye." She stopped, knowing she couldn't say more without breaking down. And then something caught her eye. At first Ellen thought it was a bold cardinal, fluttering in and out of the stand of pines that bordered the old section of the cemetery. But when she looked again, she saw that it was the tail end of a bright red scarf, caught by a stiff March wind and blown into low-lying pine branches. Ellen returned her attention to the casket mounted over the open grave. *This is it*, she thought, *Eric laid to rest with only a few of us here.*

Again, Julian nodded at the workers, and this time they slowly lowered the casket into the ground. Beside Ellen, Meg gave a little sob. Ellen held her close.

To Ellen's astonishment, a woman wearing an oversized coat ran out of the woods and retrieved the flailing scarf from the branches. Unable to contain her curiosity, Ellen released Meg and walked toward the woods. The movement did not escape Julian. Ellen sensed his displeasure, sure that Julian planned each funeral with the greatest of detail. He would consider the person in the pines an intrusion.

The woman wrapped the scarf around her neck and the lower part of her face, then ran back into the shadow of the woods. The red scarf became a tiny swatch of color before disappearing into the trees.

Julian bent and picked up a handful of dirt from the mound that had been excavated the day before. Letting the soft grains sift through his fingers, he said, "What a waste."

"Yes," Ellen agreed. "A terrible waste of a life. Eric had so much ahead of him."

"I'm talking about this soil," he said, turning his palm upward and rubbing it with his thumb and index finger. "Look how rich it is. Like gold. If the town fathers had turned this dead land into something that would be productive, like the tobacco fields over in Leighton, our economy would be booming here."

"How can you talk about business when you just buried your best friend?" Ellen stopped short of adding, *the only friend you ever had.*

Julian stared at Ellen. "Look, for more than twenty years, the only time I heard from Eric was when there was going to be a burial. First his parents' funeral and now his own." He shook his head. "You never know about people, right, Ellen?"

Aware that Meg was watching them, Ellen said, in a low voice. "That's right. You never know about people. So, is there anything else you can tell me about Eric's last wishes? As you were the last person to see him, I would hope you're not keeping something from us."

"I'll ignore that remark," he said, in a voice loud enough to catch Meg's attention. "Because I know you're upset."

Meg headed over to them. "Is something wrong?"

Ellen decided she had said enough, at least for now. Shaking her head, she looked beyond the upright granite headstone that was etched with the names of Esther and Rudolph Von Der Hyde, with the new addition of Eric's name. Julian had wasted no time in ordering the inscription.

"Maybe you can answer this question for me, Julian. Who do you think that woman was?"

Julian took off his fedora and ran his fingers through his thinning, sandy hair. "Who cares? Some vagrant, probably. We get them sometimes because the trains stop here. They don't hang around very long, not with Chief Lake in charge." Carefully setting his hat back on his head, Julian walked away.

Meg gave Ellen an inquisitive look. "What was that all about?"

"Nothing," Ellen said, turning and looking out over the steeples and monuments, to the woods in the background. She was disturbed by the woman in the red scarf, in a way she couldn't explain.

Meg sighed. "Let's go back to the house. We'll have lunch around noon. Even if Eric didn't want a real funeral, we can at least share some memories of him."

"That's a good idea," Ellen said. "I was thinking the same thing." But the truth was, she was wondering about the woman. She had the sense that the woman wasn't a vagrant, that she was there for a reason—for Eric's funeral. Had she known him? How had she found out about this burial that no one was supposed to know about?

Ellen knew she didn't have much time to find some answers, even though Marc Donovan had told her to take whatever time she needed. He had full confidence in Nick Stanton handling things in her absence. But Ellen planned to return to Boston that night. She had to get up to speed on her new job.

She turned back to her sister. "I know this is an awkward time to ask, but would you mind if I borrowed your car for a little while? There's something I'd like to check on in town. I'll pick up some sandwiches for lunch."

"No need, lunch is taken care of," said Meg, opening her purse. "And of course, you can borrow the car. I trust you still have your license, even though you don't drive in Boston."

"Oh, yes. I keep it renewed." Ellen didn't mention she couldn't afford a car even if she wanted one.

Meg handed her the keys. "I hope you don't mind driving an old Packard."

"Right now, I would drive anything," Ellen said, giving Meg a hug. "I'll drive you home first."

Over Meg's shoulder, Ellen saw Julian coming toward them. "I couldn't help overhearing you could use a ride, Meg. May I take you home? If I'm lucky, maybe you'll invite me in for a cup of coffee."

"Thank you," Meg said. "After all you've done for us, you deserve more than coffee. Just drop me off at the house, and come back at noon, for a little memorial gathering for Eric. With lunch, of course."

"I would like that very much," Julian said.

Ellen watched as Julian led Meg to his gleaming black town car and then turned to face the cemetery plots.

A certain kind of quietness had settled in. The workers had already filled the grave and were heading back to their trucks. Ellen bent down in front of the monument. With her gloved index finger, she traced the engraved lettering. *U.S. Army Major Eric Von Der Hyde 1914-1955.* A heavy sadness came over her. "Oh, Eric," she said. "What is there for us to know? Or not to know?"

She stood just in time to see the red scarf flickering to her left. The woman was running down an embankment. Ellen moved to the back of the monument. A single pink rose lay on the fresh soil.

Ellen ran to Meg's car, grabbed the heavy door handle, and almost slipped on the running board. She got into the driver's seat, inserted the ignition key, pressed her left foot down on the clutch, and moved the stick shift on the steering wheel toward her, then down, into first gear. *Meg might have had second thoughts about loaning me her car if she knew how many years it's been since I've driven,* thought Ellen, relieved that the sputtering car was moving forward.

At a fork in the cemetery road, Ellen took a right at a sign marked Serenity Lane and then another on Sky View, with elegant steeples of monuments reaching upward. In the distance, a caravan of black cars was making a serpentine line toward her. Another funeral. She backed up the car and in the rearview mirror saw the woman on the side of the road. Her knitted hat didn't cover all of her hair, which was streaked with gray. Ellen stopped the car and got out. "Wait," she called. "I only want to talk to you."

The woman turned. Her deep brown eyes reminded Ellen of an animal trapped in the glare of headlights. A workman waved his arms. "Move your car, lady," he shouted. "There's a funeral procession coming." Turning, Ellen saw that the lead hearse was only a few car lengths away. Ellen got behind the wheel of the Packard, put the gear in reverse, and backed the car up a few feet. She drove around a circular road and ended up at the rear of the caravan. When she returned to Sky View, all she could see were monuments and statues.

The woman was gone.

CHAPTER TEN

Friday, March 11

Police Chief Edwin Lake lowered his six-foot, three-inch frame into his patrol car, turned on the ignition, and drove out of the Springton Elementary School parking lot. Turning onto Main Street, he resisted the urge to blast the siren to a screaming pitch. It was lunchtime, the street was busy with pedestrians, and he was short on time and patience.

Look at you all, enjoying yourselves in this town that I spent my entire life making safe, he thought. *And I've got nothing to show for it. In a couple of weeks, I'll be nothing.* He tightened his grip on the steering wheel when he stopped at a red light in front of Oak's Tavern. Years ago, the neon sign of a whiskey bottle hanging in front of the tavern would have lured him in, but now he kept his eyes on the road. His doctor warned him years ago that he couldn't even have one drink. Alcohol wasn't good for him. It changed his behavior drastically—for the worse.

He couldn't remember when he had last felt so agitated. It was enough that his sixty-fifth birthday was next week, along with his dreaded retirement but, on top of that, his doctor had scheduled tests for a heart condition.

And now something else. *What just happened back in that class-*

room? His mind replayed the last few minutes at the school. He had gone there to meet with the principal about improving the safety drill procedures.

After, on his way down the hall, a young teacher had called to him. "Chief Lake, we have a group of pre-school children here today. They're being introduced to what kindergarten will be like for them in September. They're so excited to see a policeman. Could you please talk to them?"

He'd glanced at his watch and had said, gruffly, "I only have a few minutes."

"I assure you that's no problem," she had said with a smile. "They have a short attention span."

"All right, I'll say something about crossing the street safely," he'd said, trying to sound interested. He had followed her into the classroom.

"Girls and boys," said the teacher. "This is Chief Lake. We are very lucky to have the chief today because I've heard that he's retiring this month."

Just what I need, another reminder my days are numbered, he had thought. Leaning against the desk, he faced the class. "This school is near the corner of a very busy street, with lots of cars," he began. "There's a traffic light, with three colors that are red, green, and yellow. Here's a question." Pointing to a boy seated at a desk in the second row, he'd asked, "Young man, do you know what it means when the light turns red?"

The boy had stared, wide-eyed, at the chief's uniform. He'd pointed to the leather baton tethered to the belt. "I want to be a policeman, just like you. Can I hold that stick?"

Sighing, the chief tapped the baton. "Only a policeman can touch this," he'd said. "But I want you to pay attention and remember that the red light means for the cars to stop before you cross the street." He nodded to a girl sitting next to the boy. "And you, young lady, what happens when the light turns green?"

With a wide smile exposing deep dimples on both cheeks,

she'd said, "It's when my mommy holds my hand and we wait for the cars to go by."

For an instant, he'd had trouble focusing on the little girl's face, and he felt lightheaded. *It can't be,* he'd thought. *That Lake smile.* Those star-shaped dimples that his mother had insisted only appeared in every other generation.

Steadying himself against the desk, he continued asking each child about the colors in the traffic light while his eyes, in clear focus now, kept going back to the little girl in the second row, second seat from the right.

Nothing but a coincidence, he'd assured himself. *It has to be.*

§.

In his second-floor office at the police station, Chief Lake stared out the window. A mental picture kept sketching itself in the forefront of his mind.

The image was preposterous. He covered his face with his large hands. If there was a glimmer of a chance that his outrageous thought was possible, that meant only one thing. He, who had thought he had been so clever in plotting the scheme to the tiniest detail, had been outsmarted.

By whom, he didn't know. But he would find out. His head began to ache. With a trembling hand, he yanked open the bottom desk drawer and groped around for the only thing that would be sure to take away the pain.

CHAPTER ELEVEN

Friday, March 11

Ellen drove past the hometown shops she remembered so well: Patty's Diner, Sam's Dry Goods, and even Hal's Hardware Store, where her father had worked for most of his life.

It doesn't seem right, to take a nostalgic drive on the day of my brother's funeral, she thought, glumly. *But then again, nothing's seemed right about any of the last couple of days. And I don't have much time.* She noticed an open space in front of the police station, and slowly eased the car to curbside. She carefully went through the steps of turning off the engine without scraping the gears, then grabbed the keys from the ignition and got out of the car.

The Springton Police Station was situated on a hill, the perfect place for Chief Lake to reign over the town. Ellen had a tight grip on her shoulder bag, a reflex from years of walking in the late hours after her night classes in the city. But she relaxed her hold, reminding herself that Springton was continuously named the safest town in New England. The chief was known to be tough enough that no one would cross him, yet fair enough to earn him respect. Springton was still a small, tightly knit town. It wasn't likely a woman hovering around the local cemetery would remain anonymous for long.

ஃ

Ellen approached a desk sergeant, who was filling out reports. A portrait of Chief Lake was displayed prominently on the wall behind the desk. He was as heavy-set as she remembered him when she was in high school and he gave talks on safety. "May I speak to Chief Lake?"

Looking up, the young sergeant smiled. "Let's see if I can help you first."

"I really hoped to speak with the chief. I grew up here and I need to go back to Boston tonight. Could you please tell him that Ellen Von Der Hyde would like to see him? Just for a minute?"

He pushed a button on the phone. "Fern, an Ellen Von Der Hyde is here to see the chief. Is he available?"

After a pause, he turned to Ellen. "Sorry, the chief's in a meeting. She'll tell him you were here."

"This might sound like a little thing, but I'm trying to find a woman who seemed to be coming out of the woods at the cemetery this morning." Ellen described the woman with the red scarf.

The desk sergeant shook his head. "It's been a cold winter. A lot of people are bundled up like that. Sorry I can't be of help."

Ellen took a business card from her bag and wrote out her home phone number. "Please give this to Chief Lake," she said.

ஃ

Chief Edwin Lake's hand was now steady as he picked up the pint bottle and refilled a small paper cup with the amber liquid.

He let the whiskey trickle down his throat. It burned, and he shuddered in satisfaction. The third drink went down smoother, causing a rosy tingling sensation from head to toe.

All his pain, his ridiculous thoughts, the strange feeling in the classroom, were gone. A case of retirement nerves, he convinced himself after the second drink.

His thoughts turned to the Von Der Hyde woman. A few months ago, he had read in the local paper that she was a reporter in Boston. She must be visiting here and had heard about his retirement, which seemed to be wagging on everyone's tongues these days and was just trying to bag an interview. She probably wanted to write about the differences between a big city police chief in Boston and himself, a small-town, small-time chief. One who had only been out of New England once, to a police convention in Las Vegas.

The biggest mistake of his life. He had married a show girl.

The phone rang, and he cursed before picking it up. Grabbing the receiver, he said, "Fern, I told you I'm not available."

"Chief, there's something you might want to know. My mother just called. She heard that an old classmate of mine died yesterday. But what's strange is that the funeral was already held, right here, this morning, and I - - -."

"What has this to do with me?" he interrupted her.

"I thought you'd be interested because the man who died was Eric Von Der Hyde and, as I told you, a woman by the name of Ellen Von Der Hyde was just here, asking to see you. I wonder if her visit had something to do with Eric, that's all." Fern took a breath. "But maybe it was just a coincidence. The desk sergeant said she was trying to find a woman who was at the cemetery. Oh, I'm sorry for bothering you."

"Wait a minute," he said, as the meaning of her words penetrated his whiskey haze. "Are you saying Von Der Hyde is dead? And his funeral was in this town?"

"Yes, Chief. My mother said the arrangements were strictly private. I remember Eric was a very nice boy. His parents, Esther and Rudolph, were lovely people."

One of them was, he thought bitterly, remembering how the beautiful Esther dumped him to marry that bumpkin Rudolph. He still blamed Rudolph for losing control of his car on that rainy night four years earlier, killing them both.

"Tell me something, Fern." Lake kept his voice level. "How did your mother find out about Von der Hyde's death before I did?"

"Wendell told her," Fern replied matter-of-factly. "She ran into him at the pharmacy. And you know that sometimes he works at the funeral home in town, so he would certainly know."

"Of course," Lake said. "Thank you, Fern." He hung up the phone, stopping himself from slamming down the receiver. "Wendell must be slipping in his old age," he muttered. They'd had a deal. Wendell was supposed to tell *him* everything first, not go blabbing stuff around town.

He reached for the bottle. *A lot of this began with your big mouth, Wendell,* he thought. *Maybe things would be different today if you hadn't been minding other people's business twenty-five years ago.*

The old anger rose up in him, and he threw the whiskey bottle at the wall. The bottle smashed against a glassed-in picture of the police commissioner awarding him a certificate of commendation for community safety. Shards of glass scattered on the floor, and amber streaks of whiskey stained the oyster-white wall.

Darrel Matson, a new officer, came in without knocking. Looking first at the chief and then the wall, he closed the door. "Why don't you call it a day and go home, Chief?" he asked quietly.

"Don't tell me when to call it a day, rookie," Lake retorted. "Do you think you can tell me what to do?"

"No, Chief," Darrel said at once.

"You think I don't know the whole department can't wait until I retire? Well, you don't have to wait long. The big day is on my birthday, next week. Does that make you happy, Darrel?"

"You shouldn't feel that way, Chief."

"Don't patronize me," snapped the chief. He got up from behind his desk, his tall frame towering over the young officer. "I remember when you were a little kid, and now you think you can tell me what to do." Darrel was silent and Lake felt a twinge of regret. "Ah, heck. You're a good officer. And you're right. I'll go home, but you have to clean up here."

Darrel's face reddened, but he only said, "Yes, sir. I'll clean everything up."

"You've got many fine years ahead of you, Darrel," Lake said. "Maybe all this will be yours someday." He grabbed his hat and headed to the door. He needed to do something, anything, to forget about Eric Von Der Hyde.

CHAPTER TWELVE

Lake might have had too much to drink but he wasn't so far gone that he'd get behind the wheel like this. He dropped his patrol car keys on the front desk, grabbed a business card the desk sergeant held out to him, and refused the offer of a ride home.

He took a shortcut through backyards, like he did years ago when he'd go home for lunch. He muttered, "I don't need any heart testing. I'm as fit as those rookies."

"Hey there, Scout," he called to his neighbor's Irish setter, who barked, his tail wagging, stretching the tether that allowed the dog to run the width of the yard. Lake bent to pet him. "I'm retiring," he told the dog. "And the first thing I'm going to do is to get a dog. Just like you." Tomorrow would be a new day to think about the mess he'd made of things, a mess a million times worse than the one he just caused in his office.

He hurried through his own backyard, cursing the undergrowth and weeds that had taken over the flower gardens. He walked up the creaking steps to the back door. It had been years since he had come home this way, following the aroma to the kitchen, where she always had a hot meal waiting for him.

For eighteen years, he'd had a wonderful life, with a caring, beautiful wife. Until she began drinking again, reverting right back to the lifestyle he had taken her away from in Las Vegas.

The day she left changed him forever. He had been pouring the last of her whiskey down the sink when he'd impulsively lifted the bottle to his mouth. He was surprised that the whiskey tasted better than it had always smelled on her. And the warm glow that spread through him felt good. It made him sure that he could handle anything, even their two daughters whom she left behind.

He couldn't have been more wrong.

Enough of the past, he thought now, hurrying down the cellar stairs off the kitchen. Years ago, he had put away a pint in his office desk and another in the antique jelly cupboard in the cellar, just to prove he couldn't be tempted. But that was before he got old, before the doctor ordered all those tests, before that little schoolgirl with the dimples smiled at him.

Another drink would help him forget.

He had no idea where he had put the key, so he kicked open the cupboard door. He didn't even get the chance to search for the pint before the upstairs doorbell rang. It stopped for a second and rang again, as if someone was deliberately holding down the button. Annoyed at the long, incessant sound, he ran up the cellar steps, through the kitchen to the living room, and yanked open the front door.

Lake was momentarily blinded by a shaft of winter light that speared through the overcast clouds. "Go away," he snapped, shielding his eyes. "Whatever you're selling, I don't want any."

"I'm not here to sell you anything," said a familiar voice, a voice he hadn't heard in a very long time.

Blinking hard, he saw a woman, wearing an oversized coat with a red scarf wrapped high above her collar. She loosened the scarf.

The warm glow from the liquor immediately evaporated. Lake leaned against the doorjamb and put his hand to his forehead.

"Theresa," he whispered. "After all these years ... why, oh why, today?"

She took a step back.

He straightened and said, as calmly as he could manage, "It's cold out there. Come in."

She walked into the living room, her eyes going straight to the upright piano that hadn't been used in decades. Then, expressionless, she faced him.

My own daughter. She was in her early forties and looks sixty, he thought, seeing her matronly clothes and the salt-and-pepper hair pulled back behind her ears. There were no traces of youthful vitality in her face; her teenage beauty was long gone. *What did I do?* was his first gut-wrenching thought. *There had to have been another way.*

They stared at one another, father and daughter, like strangers meeting for the first time. He was a foot taller, so she had to look up while she searched his face. "Are you not feeling well?" she asked quietly.

"I'm fine," he said, curtly. "My doctor passed me with flying colors just last week."

A doubtful expression crossed her face, but he didn't let it annoy him. He motioned for her to sit. Instead, she took off her scarf, folded it neatly, and put it on the arm of the couch near the door.

An idea suddenly occurred to him, something that would have been unimaginable until now. All that seemed hopeless to him earlier faded away. He saw new meaning in Eric Von Der Hyde's death. His voice became animated. "Theresa, take off your coat. I just got home from the station. I need a few minutes to clean up."

In the bathroom, he quickly splashed cold water on his splotched face, gargled with mint mouthwash and combed his thinning hair in the mirror over the sink. *Damn,* he thought, seeing his badge and insignia on his white dress shirt. *I'm still in uniform.* He went into his bedroom across the hall, changed into khaki pants, transferred the contents of his pockets, and put on a plaid shirt, all the while devising his plan.

Theresa didn't know it, but she was his sole beneficiary. He had cut out his ex-wife and daughter Victoria years ago. Those two would never get the chance to squander his money in Las Vegas. And if he played his own cards right, he could take care of himself and still have something to leave Theresa.

And to hell with the doctor's tests. So what if he had one foot in the grave? His savings were more than enough to buy a small trailer. He'd drive it across the town bridge and never look back.

The ideas kept coming. Let Theresa have the house now. She always wanted to be a nurse: there were new education programs for women at the county college. She could begin all over, where she left off. And so could he.

His thoughts were interrupted by the off-key notes of the piano. He returned to the living room. Theresa, still wearing her coat, was standing at the piano, her fingers gliding across the chipped keys. "You kept the piano," she murmured. "It's a treasure chest of memories to me. The happy times, when Mom played for all of us. And the bad times."

She reached down to the piano bench and opened its tapestry-covered lid. It was empty. "Her old sheet music is gone," she said, gently closing the cover and turning to face him. "You destroyed all of it."

He had been so sure of himself, his head filled with new plans, he never thought to ask why she was here. He moved to the opposite wall and sat in a hard-backed chair, then waited for what was coming next, his body tense.

Her voice remained low. "I remember that day when you came home early for lunch, and caught Mom playing show music from her nightclub days. Victoria and I were playing dress-up, twirling around in her fancy gowns."

Theresa's brown eyes, the ones he remembered as soft as a doe's, opened wide, their centers flashing pinpoints of golden light. "You flew into a terrible rage, and she never played again. That's when she began to drink. And you drove her away. Then Victoria followed her."

So that's what this is about, he thought with some relief. Theresa was still angry about the break-up of the marriage. It wasn't a pleasant subject, but it was the least of what he had on his conscience. "And you thought today was the time to remind me of all this?"

"No. I'm here to tell you something you don't know."

"There's very little I don't know. I'm still the chief of police in this town," he reminded her gently.

"Do you remember when Eric Von Der Hyde's parents died in a car accident four years ago?"

"Of course," he snapped. "I was the first to arrive at the crash scene."

Inwardly, he was heartsick. *Beautiful Esther, dying in my arms minutes before the ambulance arrived. I could have wrung Rudolph's neck if it wasn't already broken.*

"You remember Eric came home on emergency leave from the Army for their funeral."

He gave a short nod. He'd known Eric wouldn't be staying in town long, so he had kept his distance.

"What you don't know is that the day after the funeral, Eric drove out to the old monastery. He didn't know it had become a home for the aged."

Lake tightened his grip on the chair's wooden arms. "Why would he do that? He didn't know you were there."

"That's what you wanted, to make sure Eric and I never saw each other again. You never said, but it was Wendell who caught on that I used to meet Eric in the orchard, and he told you all about it, right?"

"Yes, and he knew better than to tell anyone else." Remembering his earlier conversation with Fern, he thought, *Wendell doesn't know it, but he'll be seeing me first thing tomorrow.*

Theresa continued. "And in your rage you forced Eric's parents to send him away."

"It seemed like the only thing to do. I was trying to protect you."

"You were only thinking about yourself. You were afraid of the shame if people found out your daughter was intimate with a boy, especially one who came from a family you seemed to hate."

Lake's face darkened. "Get back to my question. Why would Von Der Hyde go to the monastery?"

"He said he had some business to attend to in the main building. Afterwards, he came around to the kitchen to say hello to Rose, the cook. He was shocked to see me there. He thought I went to nursing school all those years ago."

"And just what business brought him out there?"

"He said he went through old accounting ledgers that belonged to the monastery, but he didn't say why. He asked me to take a walk out to the peach orchard.

"And that's when I told him about my pregnancy, and that the baby, a girl, had died at birth. He begged me to believe him that he didn't know. Then he said something very odd. He said, '*That explains everything, even the wills.*' There were tears in his eyes. He asked what he could do for me.

"I asked for a memorial for our baby. I said that she deserved a marker for her grave. Eric turned so pale. Then he promised me he would make things right when he finished his military service. He said that anything he did before he went away again would make things worse for a lot of people."

Theresa stared at her father, as if seeing right through him. "And that got me thinking. First, you scared the Von Der Hydes into sending their son away to military school. But that was before I knew I was pregnant. Then, when you found out a few months later, you sent me to work and live at the monastery. But even that wasn't enough. You were so ashamed of me that you changed my last name to my middle name. Theresa Francis Lake became Theresa Francis."

Lake shrugged uncomfortably. "Maybe I didn't handle that so well," he admitted. "I'm sorry."

"My name is the least of it." She crossed her arms, her gaze cool and assessing. "I've had a lot of time to think about what Eric said—'*That explains the wills.*' I know he came back for his parents' funerals and to settle their estate. So when he read the wills he must have found something that was connected to our baby and somehow to the monastery. Why else would he go there? Now I want you to fill in the missing piece. *What else did you do to that family?*"

Lake hesitated. He never dreamed she would even have an inkling of what had gone on all those years ago. He needed to put an end to this before it all came out. He decided to tell her just enough to end her questions. "You're right. I was furious with Eric, and that's it." At the look in Theresa's eyes, he changed tack, returned to his quasi-confession. "I'll admit to having made things a little uncomfortable for Rudolph."

"A little uncomfortable?" she echoed. "What did you do?"

He shrugged again. "I had him cited for minor violations, like overtime parking, a mailbox that didn't meet code, a sidewalk that wasn't shoveled properly, petty stuff that's hardly enforced."

Theresa eyed him suspiciously. "I'm wondering if you did something more—"

"I've had enough," he interrupted, angrily. "Do you want something from me, Theresa?"

"Yes. There is a little grave at the town cemetery that needs a marker. Now that Eric is dead, I need your help to get one."

She had no idea what she was starting. *My day in hell*, he thought. He stood and ran a sweaty hand over his forehead. "You may be right about my not feeling well. Maybe it's a cold or something. Come back in a few days, and we'll talk some more."

"You're not going to help me, are you." She stated it more as a fact than a question. "Well, all right. I remember Eric had a sister. Her name is Ellen. I'll talk to her."

He rose from his chair and towered over her. "You want to talk to that nosy reporter who's fishing around town? What's wrong with you?" he thundered, regretting his words the moment they were out.

Theresa looked stricken, as if she'd been slapped. He had never laid a hand on her.

"What's wrong is that you didn't help me when I needed it most, Chief," Theresa said in a tight, controlled voice. "And it's clear that you're in no shape to help me now."

He didn't try to stop her when she turned and walked quickly to the door, not even stopping for her scarf. He took it in his hands, thinking of her last words to him. *She called me Chief. I stopped being a father the day I sent her away.*

He took the business card with the nosy reporter's name on it from his pants pocket. He needed to get to that Von Der Hyde woman.

Before Theresa got to her first.

CHAPTER THIRTEEN

Friday, March 11

Just before noon, Ellen returned to Meg's house. She found her sister in the kitchen, arranging platters of sandwiches, potato salad, and deviled eggs on the table.

Hugging Meg, Ellen said, "How did you do all this? I wasn't gone that long."

"I didn't do a thing," said Meg, "The word got around about Eric's death, and the ladies from the auxiliary made all this food for us. It's their way of giving us comfort at our time of grief."

In a soft voice, Ellen said, "That's exactly what's been missing. Friends and neighbors coming to the funeral, expressing their condolences." She sat on a high kitchen stool. "I don't understand why Eric would deny us the sympathy and support we had when Mom and Dad died. There had to be something else that was going through his head."

Meg put a Pyrex casserole dish of macaroni and cheese in the oven. "If Eric wanted us to know anything else, he could have put it in the letter. But he didn't."

"Thank you for reminding me about the letter," Ellen said, getting to her feet. "Tell me where it is and I'll get it."

Meg's eyes widened in surprise. "Why, Julian took it back for his files. I'm sure he'll let you read it if you ask."

"Julian again," Ellen said, exasperated. "How is it that he seems to be in the middle of everything?"

Meg sighed. "It doesn't seem to take much to get you annoyed with Julian. Why is that?"

"It's much more than annoyance. I resent the way he rail-roaded us through Eric's funeral, without consulting us about anything." Ellen stopped short of revealing the repulsion she was feeling towards Julian, particularly after hearing his views at the cemetery. "Let's change the subject, please."

"All right, but maybe you'd be interested to know that Julian is considered the most eligible bachelor in town."

Ellen's eyes narrowed. "Why would I care what he's consid-ered—oh," she stopped herself, suddenly understanding her sister's intent. "That's just what I need—an affair with the town mortician."

Meg's face reddened. "I didn't mean it that way. I just want you to get to know him better. To give him a chance."

Ellen gave Meg another hug. "My dear sister, I love you, but it's clear we're like night and day about Julian, and I think we should discuss him another time. Please excuse me. I'm going upstairs for a few minutes," she said, hurrying out of the kitchen.

Before Meg could say another word about Julian Baker.

Opening the door to Meg's spare room was like taking a step back into the past for Ellen, reminding her of the house she grew up in only a few miles away. Meg had arranged their parents' furniture as it had been in their own bedroom. In one corner was her father's dresser with his tarnished brass alarm clock that went off like a blast horn at six o'clock every morning. On their mother's bureau was a pottery bowl brimming over with potpourri, which gave off a scent of roses and lilacs.

Folded neatly at the foot of the bed was an afghan their mother had knitted, one of the talents Meg inherited and Ellen did not. It smelled like dewy roses, just like her bedroom when she was growing up.

Before Meg was born, she and Eric had bedrooms on the unfinished second floor. Eric's room was to the left of the stairs, hers to the right, with each doorway partitioned by floor-length drapes. Her father, the eternal procrastinator, was going to install doors someday.

Now, in Meg's house, the soft bed drew her like a magnet. She hadn't intended to lie down, but she tucked herself under the covers and closed her eyes. She heard the hum and whistle of the local train, the same sounds she used to fall asleep to when she was little, only a short distance away. Instead of lulling her into a peaceful sleep, the sounds triggered a dream.

It wasn't the night noise of the local train that awakened the little girl; it was the heavy creaking of the floorboards outside her bedroom. Through the window, an almost full moon cast its glow on a very tall man who had yanked open the drapes that hung in the doorway. The moonlight exposed only part of his face. She bolted up in her bed, too frightened to scream.

The man suddenly stepped back and let out a cry of pain. Eric had come up behind him and twisted the man's hands into a lock hold.

Eric said, "Nobody, not even you, breaks into this house. Get away from my sister."

The man said, "I was looking for you, not her. Take it easy. Let's you and I go downstairs, away from the girl. Nobody's going to get hurt."

Eric loosened his grip and turned to Ellen. In a soothing tone, he said, "It's okay now. Go back to sleep."

The little girl began to lie down, then watched in horror as the man elbowed Eric in his side, sending Eric tumbling down the staircase. She jumped out of bed and ran to the top of the stairs. Eric was lying at the bottom, his head inches from the brick hearth of the fireplace. Shaking from head to toe, she huddled behind the slats of a wooden railing.

The man's back to her, he punched Eric with heavy fists. Her father seemed to come out of nowhere and struck the man hard on his right shoulder with a fire poker. The man yelled out and writhed in pain.

Her mother was watching from her bedroom doorway, her hands covering her mouth. Catching sight of Ellen crouching behind the stair rail, she ran up the stairs and pressed the child's face into her side, covering her eyes.

"This is only a dream," her mother crooned. "This isn't happening, dear. You won't remember it in the morning." She repeated the words while she laid the little girl down on the bed, covered her with an afghan, and sat with her until she fell asleep.

❧

Ellen sat up straight from the dream, expecting to be in her Boston apartment. But instead of the blasting horns and shrill sirens of the city, there were the sounds of happy children, right under the spare bedroom window of Meg's house. And no time for Ellen to think about this dream.

She glanced at her father's clock. She'd been asleep twenty minutes. Hurrying into the bathroom, Ellen saw herself in the mirror and splashed water over her face. It was as white as the porcelain sink.

She got to the bottom of the stairs just as Beth and Matthew came bouncing through the door. They ran into her open arms and hugged her, all together in a huddle. The warmth of the children flowed through her.

Ellen laughed when Beth said, "Auntie, you smell like flowers."

Carl walked in from outside, a concerned look on his face. "Kids, you go wash up for lunch," he said. "I'd like to talk to your Aunt Ellen."

Ellen noticed tired lines around Carl's eyes. He was a quiet, mild-mannered man, an ideal husband for Meg, who wanted her young family to have a warm, peaceful upbringing, the way she'd had.

"There's something you need to know," Carl said. "The back tires on Meg's car are flat. If you had driven a few more miles, you could have had an accident."

"Both tires?" Ellen had noticed the car dragging a little on the way back to the house, but she had attributed it to her rusty skills with the stick shift, thinking she wasn't in quite the right gear.

Carl nodded. "There were nails in both of them."

"But how would they get there? I didn't pass any construction going on in town."

"It's very strange," Carl admitted. "Two nails in almost identical spots on each tire. It looked—well, deliberate."

A wind rustled up and rattled the window panes. Matthew raced into the hall and pulled at his father's sleeve. "You said we could fly our kites if it got windy, Daddy," he shouted.

Carl rumpled Matthew's hair. "Okay, son, after lunch. You can get the kites from the cellar now, though." Then, in a low voice, he said, "There's no point in telling Meg right this minute. Things are hard enough around here today without this."

"Agreed," Ellen said. "I won't say a thing about those nails."

For now, she thought.

CHAPTER FOURTEEN

In the kitchen, Meg took a baking sheet of rolls out of the oven.

"These look like homemade rolls." said Ellen, helping herself to one.

Meg smiled. "Millie Dawson brought them over." Putting down her potholders, she said, "It was nice to see you and Carl talking. He's usually a man of few words. But I know he was looking forward to having Eric be part of our family again. When you think about it, there's hardly any family left. This is it."

"Well, maybe this is enough," said Ellen. "In any case, I still want to find out the name of the woman we saw at the funeral. She left a pink rose at the tombstone."

"She did?" Meg looked surprised and then shrugged. "She's probably just a curiosity seeker."

"On this cold, windy day?" Ellen took the last bite of her roll. "No, I think she was there for a reason. And why didn't any of us recognize her? Really, Meg. Even the policeman I talked to at the station didn't know who she was. You'd think she'd attract someone's attention in this small town."

Meg's eyes widened. "You went to the police station? What were you thinking?"

"That someone should have some idea of who that woman is, but no one does," she said.

Or cares, she wanted to add.

At a knock on the back door, Meg let Julian in.

"I just knew you'd be in the kitchen," he said, handing Meg a porcelain vase with a dried flower arrangement in it.

Leave it to Julian, thought Ellen, *bringing dead flowers to a grieving person.*

She immediately felt a twinge of guilt when she saw the pleasure on Meg's face. Ellen sighed and resolved that she would make every effort to be nice to Julian.

"Oh, they're so pretty, Julian," Meg said. "This will look perfect on the corner table in the front hallway."

"That vase has been in my family for years. But it is yours now to keep, Meg. After all, we are like family."

Meg led Ellen and Julian into the living room. "Lunch isn't quite ready, so you two can talk in here. Julian, will you touch a match to that firewood?"

"Your wish is my command," said Julian. He bent to open the screen door of the fireplace.

Making eye contact with Ellen, Meg said, "A fire will make the atmosphere more cozy and warm in here. Now you two, make yourselves comfortable right there on the couch."

Behind Julian's back, Ellen shook her head. *No*, she mouthed the word. Meg nodded back with a *Yes* and left the room.

"I'll look for matches," said Ellen, opening a drawer of a lamp table.

Julian straightened up. "They'd never be in there, Ellen." He reached into a brass box on the mantle and took out a book of matches. "Meg keeps them away from the kids," he said, in a voice that implied she should have known better.

Ellen didn't know which irritated her more, his patronizing tone or that Julian Baker knew her sister's house better than she did.

She settled into an easy chair across from him. Julian sat in a half-slouched position, one leg on the couch, his gaze on the burning fire.

Just make yourself at home, she thought. Then, remembering Meg's words—'It doesn't take much for you to become annoyed at Julian'—she tried to put aside her irritation.

But Meg was so right, and Ellen wondered why. Did it go back to those Sunday dinners when, in her eight-year-old mind, she'd thought Julian replaced her? Her big brother, who once taught Ellen how to throw softballs and rode her on his bicycle handlebars, was spending that precious time with his new friend. When she had complained, her mother had said, "Julian is a lonely boy, dear. We're very proud of Eric for being a good friend to him, when no one else wants to be."

Within months, Eric was gone and it was Julian who sat across from her on Sundays, in her brother's place at the table. She remembered eating as fast as her mother would allow, then excusing herself from the table. Julian may have replaced her, but she would not let him replace her brother. Ever.

Ellen sighed, loud enough for Julian to turn and look at her. She looked away, her gaze on the spiraling flames in the fireplace, and let her thoughts continue. *Julian had been welcomed into her brother's life, her parents' home, and now he had worked his way into her sister's life and her home, too.*

And after all these years, I'm stuck with him again.

That might explain part of why she didn't like him, but not all. Her intuition told her he knew much more than he was letting on about Eric's last wishes. And she was going to do her best to find out what they really were, beginning today.

"Julian," she said, facing him. "My short drive through town today brought back many memories, and I was just thinking that it might be nice to take a ride out to the old monastery, where Eric worked. Would you drive me there, after lunch?"

Julian began to shake his head, just as Meg came into the living room.

"I heard that," Meg said cheerfully. "It's a wonderful chance for you two to become re-acquainted. Isn't that right, Julian?"

"Why yes, indeed, Meg," said Julian. But his darkening glance at Ellen belied his words.

CHAPTER FIFTEEN

The distance from Meg's house to the monastery was only twelve miles, and even with Julian driving just above the speed limit—as if he wanted to get the trip over with—to Ellen it seemed to take forever. She hadn't wanted to bombard him with questions about Eric right away and was bored silly with the small talk.

Finally, Julian pulled to the right side of the road, a few feet before the looming, wrought-iron gates. Through their pattern of leaves and scrollwork, Ellen could see a stone building set about a quarter of a mile back. "Eric worked here the summer he was sixteen and then after school, too," she said. "I was too young to remember much about it."

"There was an orchard on the property," said Julian, pointing to what looked like acres of decayed fruit trees behind the stone structure. "The monks had quite a business of making and selling jelly. Eric tended the orchard, picked peaches and apples, and even built a stone wall."

Ellen felt a wave of sorrow. Her brother, young and vital, had worked here, and now, like the orchard, he too was gone.

Julian put the car into gear and drove back onto the road.

"Wait," Ellen said. "The gates are open. Let's take a drive through."

Julian didn't hide his impatience. "Don't forget what I do for a living, Ellen. My job is twenty-four hours a day. The old people are dying off, just like these trees. I need to get back for calling hours tonight."

"But we're already here, Julian," she insisted, then added in the softest tone she could muster, "Meg would be so pleased to know we're getting better acquainted."

Taking a sharp turn, Julian drove through the gates toward the main building, and followed the road to the right, past the decaying orchard trees. Small woodpeckers chipped at the trunks, then fluttered away at the approaching car.

"They call it the Pomarium now," Julian told her. "It's a disgrace that this old monastery has been converted into a home for old people."

"Then what do you think they should have done with the property?"

"Apartments, with lush gardens. A place for the living, not the dying. The bottom line is money, more tax revenue for the town."

He eased the car through the network of narrow intertwining roads and pointed to the largest building. It was a huge stone gothic structure, with long, narrow windows and sills that jutted out under vast overhangs. Pigeons roosted on eaves. Crows cawed from high trees.

"This was called the heartbeat of the monastery, where the monks did their writing and praying," he said. "They took their meals in another building, though. Even in the worst of weather, they had to walk over to that house to eat."

He pointed to what seemed to be a smaller version of the main building. It was connected by a path to the main building, and a great chimney took up an entire wall on the north side.

"I was in that building just once," Julian said. "I was helping Eric bring in some baskets of peaches. The kitchen was huge, one of those turn-of-the-century types with a cast iron stove and ovens going halfway up the ceiling.

"There was an ulterior motive for me to help, of course," he went on, smiling for the first time. "I wanted him to get his work done faster so we could go play some hoops. I always hoped I could beat Eric one day," he said, "at least at something."

An interesting choice of words, thought Ellen. *Ulterior motive, hoping to beat Eric one day*. She wondered if there had always been rivalry on Julian's part. If there was, Ellen wouldn't have noticed it when she was a kid. Then again, maybe it wasn't anything sinister. Ellen sighed inwardly. Could it be that she resented Julian because Eric used to leave her out whenever Julian was around? Was she really carrying a grudge left over from when she was eight?

On the side of the road, two cardinals were perched on a tree branch, their red feathers a stark contrast to the gray sky. The thought of the woman wearing the red scarf flashed through Ellen's mind. She wasn't ready to let it go. There wasn't much time. Julian was driving back to the monastery entrance. Her brief tour was over.

She didn't want to annoy him. He seemed to like talking about money, so she decided she would start there and then lead into bigger questions. "So how do the residents pay to live here?"

"With whatever they have. Some of the churches support it, too. There's some tax benefits." Julian scoffed. "The bottom line is that this fertile soil is going to waste."

Dead land seems to bother him more than dead bodies, Ellen thought as Julian took a left at the gates to head back to town.

Choosing her words carefully, Ellen said, "You helped Eric when our parents died, so you must know the name of the lawyer who drew up their wills. Who was it?"

"Oh, that's old Harvey Poston. He probably won't remember much."

"Will you take me to see him?"

"I wouldn't be doing you any favors if I did. Take my word for it, Harvey can get cantankerous, especially since his wife died a few years back."

"That doesn't bother me. In my line of work, I'm used to all types of personalities. I'd really appreciate your taking me to see him."

In a terse voice, Julian said, "Maybe another time. Remember, you've got a train to catch."

"It's early afternoon," Ellen said calmly. "My train leaves at six. I want you to take me to see Harvey Poston. Now."

Julian hadn't offered a bit of information without being asked, and she was tired of walking on eggshells around him.

She decided to push some more. "And I also want to read the letter from Eric. Meg says you put it in a file."

Julian slowed the car. "If you want to see the letter, come around to the funeral home. Be sure to call first." With those words, he made a sharp U-turn in the middle of the road. Ellen noticed his knuckles had turned white.

CHAPTER SIXTEEN

Outskirts of Springton

Harvey Poston's house was in dire need of paint. A loose shutter banged against the shingles, its noise not at all disturbing a sleeping dog who didn't stir when Ellen and Julian walked past him on the porch.

A thin, frail man opened the door. He wore a frayed cardigan over a flannel shirt and baggy corduroy pants.

In a thundering voice that belied his small frame, he yelled, "I know exactly why you're here."

Ellen took a step back and the dog woke up. The old man slapped Julian on his arm. "You son of a hound dog, you're here to make sure I'm not dead yet. Don't worry, you'll get me, but only when I'm good and ready."

He laughed and then began to cough. "Come in," he wheezed. "What's the matter with you? It's cold inside, but it's a lot colder out here. You, too, Piper," he commanded, clapping his hands.

Piper grudgingly got up and followed them down a drafty hallway to a door on the right next to a worn staircase. Ellen noticed the layout of the house was similar to Meg's home.

Mr. Poston led them into a room that was lined with shelves crammed with books. The smell of kerosene came from a heater on the floor in the middle of the room. He dusted off cushions on three overstuffed chairs, gestured for Ellen and Julian to sit, then eased himself into the last one, behind a cluttered desk. "Well," he began, "as I said, I'm not dead yet. But I've got one foot in the grave. I have a rare condition, you see."

"I'm very sorry. May I ask what it is?" Ellen dropped her hand down to pat Piper, who had settled beside her chair.

"Yes, indeed you may. I'll spell it out for you. R-A-R-E. Rheumatism. Angina. Rhinitis. Emphysema." He turned to Julian. "Where's your manners, Julian? You haven't introduced me to this young lady." He put his hand up. "Never mind. Let me guess. You're finally getting married, and you want my advice on pre-nuptial agreements. Just like your father, a man who protects his assets."

Ellen bit back a smile at Harvey's emphasis on the first syllable of the word assets. Julian didn't seem amused. "This is Ellen Von Der Hyde. She has some questions about her parents' wills. They died in an accident about four years ago. I'm sure you remember."

The old man's jovial manner disappeared. "Indeed, I do," he said, so softly that Ellen could barely hear him. "A terrible tragedy." He studied Ellen's face. "I can see your determination. You're definitely not here for tea time."

Looking at Julian, he said, "It's best that you wait in the front room, near the door. There's no heat in there but you can keep your coat on."

With an exasperated look, Julian left the room, closing the door behind him.

"Thank you, Mr. Poston," Ellen said, relieved that Julian wouldn't be hovering when she asked the lawyer for information.

"Nothing personal, mind you," he said. "I don't know what

your questions are, and anything we say has to be confidential. Whatever you choose to tell him afterward is your business."

Ellen felt a tightness in her chest begin to ease. She liked the old lawyer, and for the first time, she thought she might get somewhere.

With considerable effort, he got up from the chair and went to a file cabinet. When he bent down to open a bottom drawer, Ellen could tell he was trying not to reveal the pain he was in. She wondered if it was arthritis in his back.

As if reading her mind, he said, "It's in the knees, and no, I don't need any help, thank you." Pulling out a folder, he said, "Well, here we are again. After all these years."

Ellen wondered if he was referring to finding the folder or something more.

She was hoping it was something more.

With a magnifying glass, Mr. Poston reviewed the documents at his desk and then sat without saying anything to Ellen, who sat quietly across from him. The only sound was Piper's snoring.

After what seemed like ages to Ellen, he spoke. "I should have known who you were the minute I saw you."

"How? I don't think we've ever met."

"Those distinct gray eyes. Yours are softer, like pearls. His were like silver bullets."

"Oh," she said, understanding. "I wasn't thinking that you would know Eric. But of course, he would have come here, first thing, when our parents died."

"Yes, and now you want to know about your parents' wills."

"Yes, I have questions because of some unusual things that began when Eric died."

A look of alarm crossed the old lawyer's face. "Did you just say that Eric Von Der Hyde is dead?"

"The funeral was this morning," Ellen said, her voice catching.

Taking his glasses off and rubbing his eyes slowly, Harvey put them back on and looked over at the pile of newspapers on the desk. "Then I am failing much faster than I thought. I read the obituaries every day. I don't know how I missed it."

"You didn't, Mr. Poston. There was no obituary. It was Eric's wish to keep it quiet."

The old lawyer leaned in, firing questions one after another. "When did he die? How? Where?"

Ellen couldn't help but smile. "I wouldn't want to be on the witness stand with you asking questions."

Harvey bowed his head slightly and rubbed both temples. "I may have overreacted a bit. This is shocking news to me."

"It was shocking to me, too. I'm afraid there's not much I can tell you. Eric had terminal cancer that was spreading very fast. He came back to the old hospital here to die and left Julian with burial instructions. Meg and I had no idea he was sick or that he was in the States, never mind in our own town."

"I see," he said, then sighed. "Everything that goes around comes around, doesn't it, Ellen?"

"What do you mean, Mr. Poston?"

He seemed preoccupied. "Let's just say I'm getting old." His voice drifted off. Then he cleared his throat and said, "I want you to call me Harvey. Or Harv. Now, back to business." He opened the folder. "You are aware that Eric was the executor of your parents' wills."

"Yes, Mr. Poston." At his exasperated look, she said, "I mean, Harvey."

"That's better," he said. "You are probably here for the same reason Eric met with me when your parents died. You want to know who their beneficiary was."

"No, that's in the past. Eric handled all that. I want to find out what Eric was thinking, why in the world he wouldn't let his sisters know he'd come back home to die. There's nothing for me to go on, so I thought you might know something."

"I can't pretend I understand why your brother chose to die without contacting you. This isn't the first time the Von Der Hyde family has baffled me." Harvey Poston leaned forward. "I remember the day your parents came in to change the name of their beneficiary. Your mother sat in the very chair you're sitting in. Rudolph sat right behind her. What your father lacked in talking, he made up for in being stubborn.

"I told him to go home and think about what he was doing before he signed anything, but he was adamant about not listening to one single word I had to say."

Harvey took a deep breath. "My dear, it is just as difficult for me to tell you now the terms of your parents' wills as it was for me to tell your brother Eric four years ago. Your mother and father left twenty thousand dollars of their estate to the Community Church in Keaton. It's a very large church, two towns away. That amount of money, of course, was almost all their worth, after the mortgage and other expenses were paid."

A paperweight on Harvey's desk caught Ellen's eye. It was a rough-edged stone with an etching of the monastery. Maybe that stone was part of the wall Eric helped build, she thought. She picked up the stone and held it tight. *Eric, oh, how I wish we could talk.*

"Did you hear what I said, my dear?" Harvey asked in a gentle voice.

Ellen swallowed, then said, "That isn't possible. My parents never went to services on Sundays. They certainly didn't drive all the way to a church in Keaton. Are you sure you have the right wills?"

Harvey smiled. "That's exactly what Eric said. And like I told him, my body might be going, but my mind is still intact. In my opinion, the change of beneficiary was so preposterous that I asked Esther if she were here of her own free will, and she answered with a very firm yes. At that point, Rudolph threatened to get another lawyer if I didn't do what they wanted. So very reluctantly, I might add, I honored their wishes."

He removed two documents from the folder and handed them to Ellen. She read her parents' wills slowly. Both read exactly as Harvey had said. Upon their deaths, their property and possessions, with the exception of a few jewelry pieces left to Ellen and Meg, were bequeathed to the Community Church in Keaton.

"I don't understand," she said, pushing the documents away from her. "It says here that the entire estate went to the Community Church, but Eric gave me five hundred dollars and he gave my sister the contents of their house. He said that was all that was left after he paid the mortgage, bills, and funeral expenses. Wouldn't our share have come from the estate?"

"My dear, these wills are as solid as that rock you're holding. This is the first I've heard about money or possessions given to you and your sister. Off the top of my head, I'd say that your brother may have given you the monetary gift out of his own pocket, and bought the furnishings from the estate, which he gave to Meg."

"Do you know Meg?" Ellen asked, an edge to her voice.

"I know Meg's involved in a lot of community activities, and I heard she's the best cook in town, although I've never had the pleasure of sampling her work."

With his hands on the desk, he pushed himself up out of the chair and reached for his cane. "Now, let's see if our local undertaker survived the North Pole. It'll be good for him to find out how the other half lives. It's time for my afternoon nap. You already interrupted Piper's nap, didn't they, boy?" The dog thumped his tail on the wood floor.

Harvey glanced at Ellen's hands, still clutching the rock paperweight.

"Oh, I'm so sorry," Ellen said, embarrassed. She reached to set it down.

Harvey clasped a hand over hers. "Please keep it, a reminder that you need to be as strong as that rock."

They found Julian standing in the hallway, clapping his gloved hands together. "You keep this place too cold, Harvey. Why don't you turn the heat up?"

"Because, you darned fool, you can't turn the heat up if the furnace is down," he retorted. "Do you think I like using kerosene heaters?"

Julian put his hands up. "Okay, Okay." Julian opened the front door, and he and Ellen stepped onto the porch.

"Thank you for your time," Ellen said to the elderly lawyer.

"You're welcome, but he's not," Harvey said.

"What?" Julian looked confused.

"Maybe if some of you businessmen would help some of the old people who built this town so you could have a place to get rich, we could replace our broken down, coal-guzzling furnaces," Harvey snapped.

Julian's face reddened. "How could I help you if I didn't know?"

"Well, you seem to know everything else. If you had come around to tell me this lovely young lady's brother died, you'd know."

Turning to Ellen, Harvey said, "That's Julian for you. The news is for him to know and the rest of us to find out." He slammed the door.

"Let's get out of here," said Julian, going down the stairs. Ellen stood a moment, pleased that she'd followed in Eric's footsteps. There was still a lot she didn't understand about her brother, but at least she was on the trail. And despite their unusual departure, she had a feeling that Harvey would welcome her back.

Only next time she would come alone.

CHAPTER SEVENTEEN

Friday, March 11

Boston, Massachusetts

The six o'clock train from Springton to South Station was fifteen minutes late. It had been a slow train ride, but Ellen used the time to review a folder that she had taken from the office before leaving for Springton. It was filled with information from Wayne Ellis, and even his notebook of ideas for new stories.

Now, though, that she was finally back in Boston, Ellen rushed out to the street toward a long waiting line for taxies. Night had fallen, and at the touch on her shoulder, she tightened her grip on her shoulder bag and whirled around—only to realize that it was Nick Stanton.

"You could have been a mugger," snapped Ellen. "What if I had smacked you with my bag?"

Laughing, he took her overnight case. "I watched you come through. You were in your own little world. A mugger could have easily gotten you."

"I can handle myself," she said, trying not to show her relief at seeing him.

Out on the street, the Friday night city life was coming alive.

A perfect night for a single guy like Nick to be out on the town, meeting eligible young women, Ellen thought. Instead, here he was, flagging a cab, making things easier for her.

The train ride from Springton had had an ominous feeling to it. She had been the only passenger in the car until the train came to the next stop in Madsen Falls. She had looked up from her work to vaguely notice that a few passengers had gotten on, but she couldn't shake a foreboding feeling.

"A penny for your thoughts," Nick was saying as they got in the cab.

She shrugged. "Oh, there may be a mystery going on in my family, but my sister doesn't seem to think so. I'd like to get my mind off it for a while."

"As you say." Nick pointed to a shopping bag that Meg had insisted she take home with her. "What smells so good?"

"Apple pie, meatloaf sandwiches, and corn muffins, all home-made by my sister. Why don't you come up to my apartment for a bite? There's a back entrance, so we won't disturb my landlady."

"You don't have to twist my arm. It beats the Chinese take-out I was going to offer you."

For the first time in days, Ellen felt a tinge of happiness. *I have my life back*, she thought. *Right here in Boston.*

❧

In the apartment, Ellen put the pie in the center of the small coffee table, with the muffins in a pile on one side and the sand-wiches on the other side of the pie. It didn't look right, especially compared to Meg's huge country table with cider, apples, and cheese all perfectly arranged.

Ellen rummaged through one of her packing boxes until she found a bottle of red wine and two jelly glasses. She put them in the center of the table and arranged the sandwiches and pie around the wine. She put the muffins back in the bag. "There," she said, "the muffins ruined it. That's breakfast tomorrow."

Nick took in the scene. "The table has a definite Boston flair." He rubbed his hands together. "Homemade apple pie, my favorite."

Holding the tin plate up, he turned it slowly. "I can tell this pie is a masterpiece, a culinary work of art. I've always wanted to learn how to bake a pie, not those lady pies like lemon chiffon, but apple pie, a man's pie. When things get tense, what can be a better way to forget things than to make a mound of dough, beat it down until it turns into a pie crust, then make it conform to just the way you want it?"

"Oh, stop it, please," Ellen said, trying to keep a serious face. "Just cut the pie."

He ignored her request. "And if that's not enough, look what comes next. You get to take a paring knife, peel and cut those apples, mix them with as much sugar as you like, then dump it all in the crust which, of course, you have properly pummeled into submission, then cover it all up and shove it into a hot oven."

"I'm telling you, stop."

Obviously enjoying himself, he said, "Then, best of all, you get to eat it, and your apartment smells like someone cares. There's not a soul alive who wouldn't trust someone whose kitchen smells like apple pie."

"What about the clean-up?" Ellen asked.

"What do you think women are for?"

Ellen picked up one of the balls of crumpled waxed paper from the sandwiches and tossed it in his direction. Nick deflected it, then, poised to cut a piece of pie, grinned and asked, "Can I still have some?"

"Go ahead," she said, smiling. "It's all yours."

The phone jangled. "That might be work," Ellen said with a sigh. She answered the phone. "This is Ellen Von Der Hyde."

A man with a deep voice said, "Hello, Miss Von Der Hyde.

This is Detective Malloy, at the Springton Police Department. I'm calling because our chief of police, Edwin Lake, has been hospitalized and is in serious condition. We need to talk to you as soon as possible."

"I don't understand, Detective Malloy. Will you please tell me why?"

"You were at the police station this morning, asking for the chief. You said it was about the identity of a woman with a red scarf. You left your business card with the desk sergeant. Your home number was written on the back."

"I can explain all of that."

"Let me finish, Miss Von Der Hyde. Two of our officers checked on the chief this afternoon because they were concerned about his health. They found him unconscious on the living room floor. Your business card was in his hand."

Her heart sank. "I understand. I'll be there tomorrow."

"That won't do. We need to talk to you tonight. At the police station."

"But it's too late to get to Springton. There are no more local trains." She shrugged helplessly at Nick.

Nick, who had come over to her side, whispered, "I'll drive you."

She nodded into the telephone. "All right. I'll leave as soon as I can."

"Fine. We'll be waiting for you."

CHAPTER EIGHTEEN

"Well, at least all this happened before I unpacked," Ellen said as she leaned back against the vinyl seat of Nick's blue Thunderbird. Her travel case was now in the trunk of his car.

Nick laughed as he eased the car into a traffic lane. "Here you are, about to be interviewed by the police, and all you can say is, 'At least I'm not unpacked'." He gave her a quick glance. "Am I noticing a sense of humor finally?"

"I'm so tired I must be slaphappy. Let's talk about something else." She sniffed. "Your car has a new smell to it. Not that I've ever been in a new car, of course."

"You must be wondering how I can pay for it," he said.

"That's none of my business."

"I'll tell you anyway. Just enough profits from my children's book."

The screeching noise of skidding tires made Ellen sit up, her hands groping for something to hold on to. Nick's car suddenly swerved to the right, barely missing a guardrail. His long arm stretched across Ellen as she slid forward, preventing her from hitting her head on the dashboard.

Swearing under his breath, Nick put his right hand back on

the wheel and straightened the car into the driver's lane, just as the bridge loomed before them.

"Nick, what happened?" she asked, her heart pounding.

"A car almost ran us off the road."

She looked from side to side, front and back. "But I don't see another car."

"It's speeding way ahead of us now. The car had no lights on."

"Do you think someone wanted to hurt us?"

"They could have waited until we were on the bridge, and then run us off. But they didn't. It could have just been a bad driver. Or maybe someone wanted to scare us."

'Us?' Or just me? Ellen wondered, as each mile brought her closer to Springton, the town that kept drawing her back.

Ellen took her mind off the close call with the speeding car by telling Nick about the events that led to the detective's phone call. When she finished, she said, "This all began with Eric's death. Why do you think a man who planned to retire in his hometown would shut his family out in his final hours?"

Nick's response had at first echoed Meg's, that Eric was trying to spare his sisters. He quickly changed his mind when Ellen described the terms of her parents' wills: the money originally designated to their children went to a church that directed it to a monastery. "Wow," he said emphatically. "That was a cleverly thought-out plan. You have every right to find some answers. I know I would."

Driving into Springton, Nick pointed to a rambling farmhouse set close to the road. The porch lights were bright enough to expose sagging steps and a handrail with missing slats. "My dream is to buy a house like that to restore."

"Would you buy it for an investment, to sell after it's restored?"

"Oh, no. I'd make it my home," he said. "With a wife and bunch of kids, of course."

"And a wife who bakes apple pies, right?"

"Nah, that's a man's job."

Before she could think of a quick answer, a German Shepherd, seeming to come out of nowhere in the dark night, ran out to the side of the road and barked at the car.

"And, of course, I would want a dog, and a cat, and a garden," Nick added.

"That's quite a leap from your life in Boston," said Ellen.

"Well, a man can dream, can't he?" Nick pulled into the parking lot of a motel. A neon sign blinking the name Shady Pines lit up the gravel driveway. "There's probably not too many places to stay," he said, "so I'll check in while we're here. It's only eight o'clock, enough time to freshen up. Then we'll go to the police station."

"That's a good plan. You can drop me off, and Meg or Carl will pick me up later. You've done enough tonight, and I appreciate it."

He shook his head. "I'd like to stay with you. You may need me to bail you out."

Ellen laughed, but it was a nervous, hollow sound.

Though the motel room had seen better days, it was clean. While Nick changed in the bathroom, Ellen turned the knob on the television and adjusted the rabbit ears to fix the snowy image on the small black and white screen. Not succeeding, she sat on one of the two single beds and called Meg. She was relieved when Carl answered and said that Meg was at one of her women's committee meetings.

"Please tell Meg I'll be staying overnight, but it may be late when I get to your house. I'll explain everything to her then."

She hung up the phone, ran her fingers through her hair, and glanced in the mirror over the dresser. Nick, from the bathroom doorway, was appraising her the way he had done the first time they had met, with approving eyes. Their eyes locked until she looked away.

"We have to go," she said. The huskiness in her own voice surprised her.

He cleared his throat. "You know, I really hate staying in motels alone. Why don't you sleep here? There's plenty of room," he said, gesturing to the two beds.

She forced a laugh. "That's not a good idea. The townspeople have enough to gossip about already."

He moved a step closer to her. "We can have a nice dinner, and maybe some wine."

Her tiredness eased enough to clear her thoughts. There was no doubt she was losing control. She stared at him hard, at the ironed white shirt he had changed into and the dark blue tie that he had put around his collar but hadn't yet knotted. She resisted the urge to put her hands out and knot his tie. She was sure her knees were quivering. There must be dozens of women who wouldn't mind being alone with Nick Stanton on a Friday night.

My God, she thought. *What am I doing in a motel room with someone who works for me? And why haven't I asked him about what's been happening at work?*

She took his sports jacket off the hanger and handed it to him. "Let's go," she said, ignoring his questioning look.

CHAPTER NINETEEN

The police station was almost as busy as South Station, Ellen thought. Local reporters were waiting for any kind of breaking news about the condition of the police chief. Nick dropped her off and went to find a parking place.

A night duty police officer, with tired lines crossing his face, did a double take when Ellen made her way through little groups of people who were talking in hushed tones.

"Hello, Ellen Von Der Hyde. If I didn't know you were coming in, I'm not sure I would have recognized you. You look wonderful. Boston life must agree with you."

"Hello, Bruce King," she said, recognizing him immediately. "I had heard you and your brother Jeremy were police officers." Glancing at his badge, she said, "You're a sergeant now. Congratulations."

Taking her aside, he said, "You're here to see the detectives, but first, I want you to know I heard about Eric only this morning. Maybe I could have helped somehow if I had known."

"That's very nice of you, but there wasn't really anything you could have done."

"I feel that I owe him. You may remember that when Jeremy

and I were kids, we were headed for trouble. Then one day we had a big awakening. There was Eric, winning sports awards, getting good grades, and there we were, maybe just steps away from being hauled through these very doors for delinquent behavior," he said, nodding to the front door of the station. His voice trailing off, he said, "We never would have made it to police academy if we hadn't started looking up to Eric as our role model, that's for sure."

"I appreciate your sharing that with me," said Ellen, learning one more thing about her brother. "Thank you."

Bruce smiled at the memories. "And who could forget what Eric did for poor Julian when he was a kid."

"Ah, yes. Julian," said Ellen. "He was very much in our lives."

And still is, she thought, following Sergeant King down a long corridor.

❧

A very curt detective stood at the door of a smoke-filled room. "Thank you for coming in," he said. "I'm Detective Malloy and this is Detective Lewis." He nodded to a middle-aged man, his white shirt sleeves rolled up, seated behind a desk with an open folder in front of him. Detective Lewis, with a grim look on his face, held a telephone receiver in one hand, a cigarette in the other. He put the phone receiver in its cradle and crushed the cigarette on a heap of smoldering stubs in a metal ashtray.

Leaning back in a wooden swivel chair, Detective Lewis pointed to a hard-backed chair in front of the desk. "Please sit, Miss Von Der Hyde. First of all, I'm sorry about the death of your brother, and that you had to come all the way back here. This has been a long day, and it's going to be a longer night, so I will get straight to the point." Drumming his fingers on the desk, he said, "I am sad to say that our chief of police, Edwin Lake, passed away minutes ago."

Ellen was as still and straight as the chair she sat on, her thoughts whirling like the wisps of smoke from the ashtray. The detective leaned forward and continued. "We have been told that Chief Lake became very upset this morning, around the time he heard about your brother Eric's death. This happened right around the time you visited the police station asking about a strange woman at Eric's funeral. Coincidence?"

Her eyes began to water from the lingering cigarette smoke. "Detective Lewis, I have no idea. I wish I did." Detective Malloy handed her a box of tissues. Ellen wondered if he thought she was crying. But she was way beyond tears. "Thank you," she said, taking a tissue and dabbing her eyes.

"All right then," Detective Lewis went on, "it comes down to this. Either the chief died of natural causes or by foul play. Until an autopsy is conducted, we must examine all possibilities."

Still watching her, he shook a cigarette out of a crumpled package and rubbed it between the thumb and index finger of his left hand. Ellen turned away from his gaze and focused on the cigarette, trying to anticipate what the detective was leading up to. There had to be more than this to bring her back here. She coughed. He put the cigarette down.

"Our Chief of Police was found lying on his living room floor, barely breathing. There were two important items at the scene. As I told you on the phone, your business card was clutched in his hand. That's one item."

His next words stunned her. "And right beside him, on the floor, was a scarf. A red one," he said, reaching into a desk drawer and pulling out a plastic bag containing a red scarf. "Does this look familiar?" he asked.

Ellen chose her words carefully. "It's about the same color as the one I saw in the cemetery, but I don't know for sure. I'd say there's a possibility."

The detective fired questions at her. Questions for which she had no answers. No, she had no idea whom the woman was. No, she couldn't think of anyone from Springton that her brother kept in touch with. Not even Julian Baker, his childhood friend.

"Interesting that you mention Julian," said Detective Malloy, stepping closer to the desk. "Julian, our town undertaker, who kept Eric's death so private that there seemed to be a shroud of secrecy around it. Very unusual for him, to bypass professional courtesy procedures."

"What procedures?" Ellen asked, suddenly intrigued.

"There's a reason that Springton is known for its low crime rate. And that's Chief Lake's tight rein on most things that go on in town. Funerals can attract all kinds of people, from other areas."

At Ellen's curious look, he said, "If we know there's a funeral, we can prepare for concerns like traffic issues, since funeral processions have priority and are allowed to go through red lights. And sometimes we drive by people's houses when they're at the funeral of a family member, just to check."

"Yes, I've heard of a rash of house break-ins during funerals. People sometimes put too much personal information in obituaries," Ellen said, making a mental note to do a story.

Detective Lewis nodded, then stood. "Right now, we've got to give a statement to the reporters about the chief's death. Where we go from here, depends on the autopsy. If the chief died of natural causes, we most likely won't contact you again. But if it's a suspicious death, then there's no doubt you will be called in," he said, pulling on his suit jacket that was draped over his chair. "Have a safe trip back to Boston and be careful no matter where you are. As Chief Lake used to say, 'city problems have a way of trickling to the small towns'."

৪৯.

"Ah, no handcuffs, I see," said Nick, opening the car door for Ellen. "How did it go?"

"Well, there may be new importance to the fact that I visited the police station and asked to speak to Chief Lake about the strange woman."

"New importance?"

"The chief died a short while ago." Taking a deep breath, she added, "And he was holding my business card, and that's not all ... there was a red scarf next to him."

Nick gave a low whistle. "I'd like to use some strong language here, but I'll just say, *Holy Smoke*."

"That says it all," Ellen assured him. "Everything around here seems to be going up in smoke."

CHAPTER TWENTY

On the way to Meg's house, Nick wanted to hear every detail about Ellen's interview with the detectives. She recapped everything, almost word for word, but when she was done, he just kept his eyes on the road, seeming content to drive in silence. She gave him a long look. "What are you thinking about?"

"I'm mulling over what you've told me, and how right you were in pursuing the woman's identity. There's something really off there."

Ellen relaxed against the seat back. "Thanks, Nick. It helps to hear that."

"You know," Nick said, "when you were in there with the detectives, I wasn't the only one waiting for you. That Julian guy doesn't seem to miss a thing."

A chill snaked up Ellen's spine. "Julian was waiting for me? How did you ever recognize him?"

"I didn't. I heard Sergeant King say to a guy at the desk, 'No, you can't see Ellen right now, Julian.' Then he pointed to me and said, 'Maybe her friend over there will talk to you.' Julian seemed surprised."

"Surprised because I have a friend?"

"Maybe he has a thing for you and was afraid I was your boyfriend."

Ellen laughed. "Julian does not have a thing for me, nor for anyone else as far as I know. He's a completely self-absorbed person."

"Anyway, we made introductions."

"Then what?"

"Would you believe me if I said I told him that you and I were sharing a room at the Shady Pines?"

She shook her head and grinned. "No, I wouldn't, and besides, I don't much care what Julian thinks."

"Mind telling me more?"

"It's just what I told you when we drove up from the city. Julian was the last person to see Eric alive. Eric somehow sent word for him to go to the hospital. But Julian refuses to tell us anything more about that visit. My sister sees nothing wrong with this, and for the first time in our lives, we are having differences. She sees all these wonderful qualities in Julian, and I don't."

A lamplight glowed in front of a house on the right. "There's Meg's house," she said. "Just pull into the driveway."

"This one?" asked Nick, slowing down in front of a house with a picket fence.

"Yes. And no dogs coming out at you and barking. My sister would think that would be terribly rude."

Nick grinned. "Touché."

A room in the back of the house was lit. Meg was waiting up for her in the kitchen. *She's her mother's daughter*, Ellen thought.

Nick walked her up the wood stairs of the wraparound porch. "Another wonderful, New England home," Nick said. "If the weather were warmer, we could sit for a spell and enjoy a pitcher of lemonade. I think I'd like that. Is this the house you grew up in?"

The cold night air felt good on Ellen's face after the stuffy police station. When she spoke, her exhaled breath looked like dandelion puffs against the lamppost. "No. It was Carl's mother's house. Mrs. Anderson lived with them for a year before she died. They took very good care of her. It's sad she didn't get to see her grandchildren. Matthew was born right after she died. Then our parents died when Meg was expecting Beth. My poor sister hasn't had it easy."

"You haven't had it very easy, either," Nick murmured.

Remembering earlier, when he reached out for her hand, Ellen wondered what it would have been like to have his long arm around her. Or what it would be like now to have both arms holding her. Ellen forced herself to stop thinking about Nick's many charms. As he moved closer, she pointed to a street sign.

"That's Myrtle Road. To get to the house we grew up in, you drive a couple of miles, pass some farmland until you come to an unpaved road that's lined with lilac trees. Our address was One Lilac Lane. If you come in the spring, the fragrances of the lilacs will knock you over. There must be a hundred lilac bushes."

Nick was so close she could smell his shave lotion, a faint woodsy scent that she had never noticed in Boston.

"Is the house on Lilac Lane as big as this one?"

Ellen laughed. "Far from it. It's a bungalow. Really, the house was like a doll house. Eric and I had tiny bedrooms on the unfinished second floor. By the time Meg was born, Eric was away in military school, and it's a good thing, because there would have been no room for her."

The hallway light flickered on. Ellen laughed; it was something else their mother used to do. "That's Meg's signal for me to go in the house, my curfew. Why don't you come for breakfast at eight tomorrow and we'll be on the road by ten?"

"Are you sure Meg and her husband won't mind?"

"I'm positive. Meg always makes country-style breakfasts on the weekends. And take my word for it, she'll be sending us back to Boston with another bag of wonderful food."

"That does it. I'll be here," he promised.

Ellen watched Nick go down the porch stairs and smiled when he turned and gave her a thumbs-up sign. She opened the front door and walked quietly down the hallway to the kitchen. Meg was sitting at the table, a low lamp shedding light on a plate of sugar cookies. Ellen gave her a hug and sat down across from her. She took a cookie and nibbled on it.

"I'll get you some milk," Meg said, getting up from her chair.

"No," Ellen said, reaching across the table and taking her sister's hand. "Meg, we have to talk. Don't you want to know why I'm back in Springton at this hour?"

"I know all about it," Meg answered indignantly.

"How would you know why I had to come back?"

"Julian told me."

"Of course," Ellen said. "How could I not have guessed?"

Speaking in clipped tones, Meg said, "Julian said the chief may have died in a suspicious manner, and you were called in for questioning. Ellen, I don't like any of this. I'm raising a family here."

"But your family won't be affected, Meg. I'm the one who was snooping around, trying to learn more about that woman. The detectives wanted to talk to me, not you."

"I just don't like thinking of that woman hovering around our family plot." Meg shuddered, then crossed her arms in front of her chest. "What's that old saying? That when you shiver it means someone is walking on your grave?"

Ellen looked directly at Meg's clear blue eyes. "Are you frightened of something?"

Meg looked down and smoothed the fringes of the woven tablecloth. "Maybe. I just don't see why this woman is so interested in our family graves. Remember, the cemetery is only a mile from this house. It's creepy."

A chill went up Ellen's back. She had been out in the cold night air too long. She drummed her fingers on the table. "Well, maybe there is someone walking on our graves, Meg. Maybe there is."

The woman's figure was almost indistinct against the waning moon sky. She moved hesitantly through the aisles of tombstones until a stream of light cut through the moving clouds, and then she moved surely and swiftly, her boots making a crunching sound on the hard ground.

She found the granite tablet that was glistening with ice crystals and knelt. The clouds passed across the moon, bringing a curtain of darkness down on her. She ran her fingers gently along each name on the stone, stopping when she came to the last line. When the moon again revealed part of itself, she read the name of Eric Von Der Hyde. The woman pressed the left side of her face against the stone, hard enough to feel the imprint of the etching on her cheek, and then quickly withdrew it, shocked by the coldness of the stone.

She put her hand in a pocket of her oversized coat and took out a rose. It was already frozen, so she crumbled the petals and scattered them on the ground. "*Sed non culpa mea est*," she murmured. "But the blame is not mine." She stood and followed the beam of moonlight back the way she had come. When she got to the woods, she opened her mouth and wailed, and the sound was carried by the wind to the top of an oak tree where an owl matched it with a mocking screech.

CHAPTER TWENTY-ONE

Saturday, March 12

While Meg was busy helping the children get dressed, Ellen flipped through the pages of the family photo albums in the living room. To her disappointment, there was no mysterious woman. She recognized all the faces.

Carl came in with a stack of wood to add to the fireplace to ward off the cold wind rattling the windowpanes.

"'Morning, Carl," Ellen said as she watched her brother-in-law stack the wood next to the hearth. "I've been wondering if you found out any more about those nails in the tires?"

He stood and brushed off his jeans. "Just that the nails were shiny, like new."

"What does that mean?"

"Meg said you went to the police station. Hal's hardware is nearby. They sell nails there by the pennyweight. Someone could have come out of the shop, dropped a bag of nails, and didn't pick them all up."

"And you think that's what caused the two flats?" Ellen asked.

Carl shrugged. "Right now, it's the best explanation I've got."

"Did you tell Meg about the tires?"

Carl nodded. "She said she doesn't want to think about what could have happened."

It's not the only thing she doesn't want to think about, Ellen thought, realizing she was learning more about her sister every day.

They both turned at the sound of a knock at the front door. Ellen glanced at her watch. It was just past eight. "I'll get it," she said, and started for the door, but Meg, coming downstairs with the children in tow, reached it before her.

Meg let Nick in. Ellen made the introductions and smiled when Nick presented a giant bag of unshelled peanuts to Meg.

"Something for the kids," he said, then added apologetically, "There was nothing open in town last night, except the lounge at the motel."

Meg smiled warmly. "Why, thank you, Nick. This is a wonderful treat for them."

Ellen helped Meg set the table while Nick joined Carl and the children in the living room. Within minutes, they heard sounds of laughter. "Is Nick always this noisy?" Meg asked.

"I think lively is more like it. Here, let me help," Ellen said, unwrapping a stick of butter and plopping it down on a saucer.

"I guess he's a typical Bostonian," Meg said, taking the saucer from Ellen's hands and sliding the butter onto a glass butter dish, then slicing it into little square pats.

Meg reached into one of the cupboards and took out a china dinner bell, then shook it. The noise in the living room drowned out the tone of the bell. Meg put it down and walked to the doorway, hands on her hips.

"Breakfast. I'm not calling you again," she said.

Meg had the same broad shoulders and almost the identical stance as their mother, Esther. And those flowery bib aprons. *How do you tie a perfect bow behind your back?* Ellen wondered.

At the table, Beth and Matthew insisted on sitting on either side of Nick. While Meg served platters of pancakes, sausages, and bowls of homemade applesauce along with fried potato slices, Nick entertained the children with stories of Boston.

"You must come to Boston," he said. Giving Ellen a warm look, he added, "When the circus comes to town, maybe Auntie Ellen and I can go with you and your mom and dad."

Carl nodded. "My parents took me to the circus when I was ten. I'll never forget it. That's a good idea, Nick."

A look of shock crossed Meg's face. "How can you think of such a thing, Carl?" she asked. "The city's no place for children. Let's change the subject, please." Smiling at Nick, she said, "If Beth had been a boy, we were going to name him Nicholas, and, of course, call him Nick."

Nick, pleased at the compliment, went into a dissertation about the generations of men in his family with the name of Nicholas. He ended with the lamentation that, alas, since he had no siblings, he was the end of the line.

Ellen guessed what was coming. *You wouldn't,* she thought.

But he did. "The responsibility is now solely mine," he said, "to carry on the family name of Nicholas."

Ellen was aware of Meg's eyes on her while Nick talked. *Remind me to thank you, Nick,* Ellen thought.

Returning her sister's stare, Ellen asked brightly, "May I have more applesauce, Meg? It's the most delicious I've ever tasted."

"Of course, my dear," responded Meg in the same tone, her eyes twinkling. "Would you like to have the recipe?"

Beth chimed in. "It's easy, Auntie Ellen," she said. "You just put the apples in a big pan of water and cook them until they're all mushy."

"That reminds me, Beth," said Nick, turning to the little girl. "I would love to learn how to bake an apple pie, like your mother makes. Can you tell me how to make one?" Beth shrugged her shoulders and then giggled when Nick turned to her brother. "How about you, Matthew, do you know how to make an apple pie?"

Matthew was busy mopping his pancakes in maple syrup. "I don't know," he said. "I guess you make a big ball out of the dough and dump apples in it, that's easy."

While everyone laughed, Nick directed his gaze at Ellen and said, "That's exactly what I thought."

Ellen was sure her heart was pounding as loud as Nick's earlier knock on the door.

֍

At Meg's insistence, Ellen and Nick took their coffee into the living room. Ellen set her cup and saucer on the coffee table while Nick rubbed his hands together in front of the fire in the fireplace.

"I haven't even asked you about work," she said. "I hope Nigel took photos of the old neighborhood that a councilman wants to have razed. It will be a great feature story."

"Those photos didn't happen," he said, turning to face her.

"What do you mean?" asked Ellen.

"Wait till you hear this," Nick said, excitement in his voice. "There were a couple of guys who were scaling one of the high-rise buildings. I had Nigel take photos."

"But what they were doing is illegal."

"Of course, it's illegal. But that's where the crowd had gathered. Nigel took photos of the police getting them down."

Ellen spoke slowly and deliberately. "Nick, the feature story was supposed to highlight the changes that are being talked about that will affect a small community, not about some guys who are risking their own lives and maybe others', for goodness sake. Marc Donovan must be absolutely furious that you allowed this."

"Ellen, that story can be done another time. This was for the moment. And don't worry about Marc Donovan. He's ecstatic," Nick assured her. "Wire services picked up the photos."

Ellen listened to the ticking of her parents' grandfather clock in the hall. She smelled the wood smoke from the fireplace mingling with the coffee aroma from her cup. She heard Meg working in the kitchen, opening and closing the refrigerator, cleaning up after one meal, preparing for the next. *Meg has the life she wants right here,* Ellen thought. *But it isn't mine. All that's happened here in the last few days has consumed me and taken over my own life—and possibly my job.*

Her eyes fell on Nick. *And last but not least, why in the world am I responding to Nick's attraction to me? He isn't hiding his feelings, that's for sure. Maybe some distance will be good for both of us.*

She got up from the couch and walked over to Nick. "I appreciate all your support and especially you driving me here, but I've decided not to go back to Boston today. Actually, I may be here through most of Monday. There are some things I need to check out in Springton. If I don't find some answers soon, I'll be going back and forth forever. It would be best if you left now so you can prepare for Monday."

Nick gave her a knowing smile. "You're doing this because you think I usurped your authority, isn't that really it?"

"Not at all. The truth is that you're capable of doing the job in my absence, and that's what teamwork is all about. That's what Mr. Donovan needs and wants. There's a financial planning meeting scheduled for Monday, and I'm confident that you can make the presentation to the officers."

"Are you kidding? When did you get a chance to write up a financial presentation?"

"Wayne Ellis had the report almost completed. I just needed to call the accountants for some numbers, and I called it into Brenda late yesterday afternoon. She should have it all typed up by now. You just need to check it against the original for any errors, then have Brenda make carbon copies. The meeting is at two, so you'll have plenty of time. I'll call Mr. Donovan later to explain I need another day or two here."

Meg came into the living room. She was carrying a shopping

bag, which she handed to Nick. "Here are some sandwiches for you two." Giving Ellen a puzzled look, she said, "But did I really just overhear you say that you're staying another night?"

"Yes, maybe two." Ellen sent Meg a message with her eyes to not pursue the line of questioning.

Meg got the message. Giving Nick a hug, she said, "I's been so nice to meet you, Nick. And thank you for the bag of peanuts. We'll play hide the peanut at Beth's birthday party next week."

"I can't remember when I've felt so much at home," Nick told Meg. "You and Carl have a wonderful family. Beth and Matthew are great kids."

"Thank you," she said. "I hope you'll visit us again soon."

Before Meg could say anything more, Ellen said, "Meg, please get me some pencils and the biggest sketch pad you have. I'll see Nick out.

"And Nick," she said, heading to the hallway. She reached for her bag and pulled out a small notebook. "I've been going through Wayne's notes. He was setting up several interviews for the rest of March." She ripped out a page and handed it to him. "The contact information is all here. Please follow up."

"Yes indeed, Madame Editor," he answered.

Ellen opened the door of the hall closet and pulled Nick's jacket off the hanger. From the top shelf, a ball of red yarn with two knitting needles sticking out of it caught her eye. She closed the closet door and held the jacket out to Nick. "Good-bye, Nick. Call me with any questions." She pulled open the front door.

Nick shook his head and walked down the porch stairs without looking back.

In her haste to open the closet door again, Ellen knocked over Julian's dry flower arrangement. The vase was still in one piece, with the dried flowers, now shreds of confetti, spilling across the floor.

Meg hurried down the stairs. "What's going on?"

Ellen pointed to the ball of red yarn. "What is that?"

"That's the beginning of a scarf that I'm knitting for the school bazaar for next Christmas. I make them every year."

"Then it's possible that woman may have been wearing one of your scarves?"

Meg put her hands on her sister's shoulders. "I'm getting worried about you, Ellen. There must be thousands of red scarves in this world. I really think you should go back to Boston with Nick. That is, if he's still speaking to you."

Ellen gave her sister a wry smile. "I'm sorry. I'll try not to overreact. Can you please get me the pencils and pad?"

Meg sighed and headed back up the stairs. "I can guess what you want them for. I wish you'd let me teach you to knit instead."

To Ellen's relief, Meg hadn't seemed to notice the vase that had rolled into the corner of the hallway. She quickly scooped up the crumbles of dried petals and shoved them into the vase. With any luck, maybe Meg would think they had just disintegrated.

Ellen pressed so hard on the paper that the pencil tip broke. With a fresh pencil, she drew a woman's heart-shaped face. She sketched a knitted hat that covered all of the woman's hair to the ears and then added a wave of hair on her forehead above her left eyebrow. She drew a scarf which covered her cheeks and nose.

Taking another piece of paper, she made an identical sketch. She saved the eyes for last.

Going back to the first sketch, she made the eyes wide and alert. On the second, she showed eyes wide with fear.

Across the table, Meg was snipping the ends of string beans with kitchen scissors. "I didn't know you were going to stay over," she said, looking up. "So, when Julian arrives, I don't want you to think I invited him just because you're here. He often has dinner with us on the weekend.

"I really don't know what you have against him," Meg went on, putting the scissors down. "He did so much for us when Mom and Dad died. After all, you and Eric didn't care."

Ellen dropped the pencil. "What are you talking about, Meg?"

Meg raised her voice. "My own brother and sister, coming home for two days and then leaving the day after our parents are buried. Leaving me. That's what I'm talking about."

"But Meg, Eric had to get back to Germany, where he was stationed at that time. And I offered to stay, but he persuaded me to go back to college. It was during exams, and I was holding down two jobs. I needed every penny I could get for tuition."

"That can't be true. You had all the money you needed, maybe even more, from Mom and Dad's estate."

Stunned, Ellen said, "I don't know what you mean. I received five hundred dollars and you got the contents of their house. The rest of their money went for bills, funeral expenses, and the mortgage. Eric handled all of that for us."

"You only got five hundred dollars? Oh, please. I was married, so I thought Mom and Dad figured I was taken care of, and that's why I only inherited the furniture. I've tried not to let it bother me, but I'm the one with a family. I want Matthew and Beth to go to college, just like you did." Tears streamed down Meg's cheeks. "Carl's tool business isn't doing as well with all the big stores going up in the nearby towns. And you can see for yourself this house needs work. The windows need to be replaced, and the furnace is on its way out."

Ellen's mind was racing with alarm. "Listen to me, Meg. I'll show you my bills and my receipts, the loans I had to pay, and even my old pay stubs. And if that isn't enough, let me ask you this: Why did it take me seven years to complete a four-year degree? Do you think I worked my way through by choice? And to say nothing about the gambling debts my ex left me."

Ellen shook her head. "I might not have graduated at all if it hadn't been for the few hundred dollars that Eric gave me." She reached into her shoulder bag and took out her billfold. "I'm living from paycheck to paycheck. You can see for yourself. I have twenty dollars until next week."

Meg turned away. "I don't need to see it. I'm so sorry," she said softly.

"But for four years, you thought that I had something that should have been yours, too."

Meg took a tissue from her apron pocket and blew her nose. "I've been so busy. I really haven't thought about it, until now. Something seems to be very wrong, and I don't know what."

Ellen put her arm around her sister. "There's something I need to tell you. Let's sit some more."

Meg wiped her hands on her apron, and they sat closer to one another at the table. Taking Meg's hands in hers, Ellen said, "You know that Julian took me to see Mom and Dad's lawyer, Harvey Poston, but I didn't tell you everything he told me."

"Why not?"

"I wanted to check out some things first, but now that I know how you've been feeling, it would be so much better to get everything out in the open and work together. Will you help me, Meg?"

"I don't know how much I can do, but I'll try."

Ellen recapped her conversation with Harvey, how she read their parents' wills and found out exactly what Eric, as executor, learned four years before. Rudolph and Esther Von Der Hyde had bequeathed their estate to the Community Church in Keaton. Eric, Ellen, and Meg were not named as beneficiaries.

"Then how did I inherit the furniture and you received tuition money?"

"I asked Harvey that very same question. His guess is that Eric bought the furniture from the estate for you and gave me money from his own pocket."

Meg shook her head. "This is unbelievable. I don't know what to say."

"Meg, you and I never had a chance to grieve together. I can see that now. But let's try to find some answers to our questions."

Meg nodded. "All right," she said in a low voice.

Ellen spread the sketches on the long table. "Here," she said gently. "Does this face look familiar to you?"

Meg studied the sketches. "Not at all."

Ellen rolled up the sketches. "I have a plan. Tomorrow morning, we'll go to the high school library to look at some old yearbooks. But, oh no, we can't," she realized. "Tomorrow is Sunday. The school will be closed."

"We'll be able to get in anyway," said Meg. "The librarians and volunteers are getting ready for the April book fair."

Meg looked thoughtful. "But Carl and I need to go over our taxes tomorrow for our appointment with the accountant next week. So you take my car, and Carl will drop me off later at the school. We'll meet in the library."

Ellen couldn't hide her excitement. "Oh, I appreciate this so much. And after we go through the yearbooks, I'd like to drive out to the Community Church in Keaton and talk with the pastor there."

Meg shook her head. "I can't imagine what would make our parents leave all their money to a church in another town."

"Neither can I," Ellen admitted. "But I'm going to do everything I can to find out."

CHAPTER TWENTY-TWO

Sunday, March 13

A snow squall, seeming to come out of nowhere, spread a layer of snow against the windshield just as Ellen drove through the main entrance of the cemetery. She was on her way to meet Meg at the high school, but on an impulse, had taken a turn to the cemetery. She put on the window wipers, but they were sluggish and made the visibility worse. She pulled over to the side of the road about fifty feet from her family's plot and dusted off the windshield with a snowbrush she found in the back seat.

The squall passed, leaving in its wake a dusting of white snowflakes. At Eric's grave, Ellen saw the woman. Her heavy coat hung unevenly, just above her boot tops. She was facing the tombstone, standing as still as the statues.

Ellen got out of the car, certain the woman had heard the engine turn off and the car door close. Moving carefully, she began walking toward the woman. "Hello there," she said, stopping a few feet from the grave, hoping she wouldn't run off.

The woman pointed to the tombstone. "The baby's name should be on here," she said, turning. Her eyes were level with Ellen's now and similar to those in Ellen's sketch. They were large brown eyes that revealed vulnerability, eyes that belonged to someone who may have been the student of rejection and who could now be its very teacher.

"Baby? There's no baby here," Ellen said gently. "Just my parents and brother, no one else."

"The baby is here," the woman insisted, hardly moving her lips when she said the few words.

"Maybe I can help," Ellen said. "You're probably at the wrong plot. If you tell me who you are, we'll go to the caretaker's office and look up the name you're searching for."

The woman shook her head. Ellen reached into her bag and took out a pen and her business card. She wrote her home address and phone number on the back.

"Here's my name," she said, pressing the card into the woman's hand. "Now please tell me yours."

The woman's eyes darted to the business card. She said nothing.

"And your name?" asked Ellen. *Please tell me your name.*

The sounds of an approaching car startled the woman. She looked the same way she had the first time Ellen had seen her. Fearful. Trapped. It seemed to be an effort to move with the weight of her coat, but she walked away, slowly, to the other side of the tombstone and down the embankment.

On the gravesite lay a single pink rose dotted with tiny snowflakes. Under the rose, which was already dying, was a piece of paper. Ellen picked it up and read the words, "Baby Girl Rose" in scroll-like penmanship. She looked down the embankment. The woman had disappeared into the woods. Again.

I'm not going to follow you, poor thing, Ellen thought. *I have a feeling we'll meet again. On your terms, of course. But at least you know who I am. And you may even be starting to trust me.*

CHAPTER TWENTY-THREE

Meg was sitting at a table in the library. "I just got here myself," she whispered.

"How did you and Carl do with the taxes?" Ellen whispered back.

Meg grimaced. "We'll know for sure when we see the accountant, but it looks like we owe income tax this year. At least we have until April fifteenth. I'll worry about it later. Meanwhile, you and I have work to do."

Meg pointed to two stacks of yearbooks. "I called ahead and asked the librarian to put these out for us."

"I'm very impressed, Meg," said Ellen.

"Well, the librarians know very well who runs the bake sales to raise money for new books."

Ellen smiled. "Why Meg, that's the way we talk in the city."

"Oh no," Meg answered, putting her hands up in mock despair.

They sat on hardwood chairs that Ellen remembered from her days at the school. The yearbooks gave off a musty smell.

"Where do you want to begin?" asked Meg, taking Ellen's sketch and unfolding it. She smoothed it down on the table.

"How about starting with the most recent yearbook and working back?"

"I don't think so," said Ellen, thinking of the woman she had just seen at the cemetery. She would bring Meg up to date later. "Actually, she may be older than I thought. Let's start thirty years back."

Meg rearranged the books, removing the most recent ones and stacking the rest chronologically. Ellen took a pencil and worked on the sketch. She added line marks around the eyes when a sudden thought occurred to her. "Darn," she said, tapping her pencil hard on the table. "I almost missed it."

"What?" asked Meg, startled.

Ellen quickly decided that it wasn't the right time or place to tell Meg that she had talked with the woman. "I stopped at the cemetery on my way here. The woman was at the grave but she wasn't wearing the red scarf. That may mean something."

Meg sighed. "What that means is that she simply didn't wear a scarf today or she wore it inside her coat, so it didn't show. Now can we please get on with this?"

Meg opened an old yearbook with a dog-eared cover. "Here, take a look." She pointed to the top picture on the first page. A young man with freckles across his nose smiled widely, revealing braces across crooked teeth. "Bob Anderson," she said. "He's Carl's brother. Now I know where Matthew gets his overbite." She gave a rueful laugh. "We'd better include braces for Matthew in our rainy-day fund."

Half an hour later, they had gone through only a few yearbooks. Meg was intrigued with the photos and when she came across someone she recognized, she stopped to tell Ellen what she knew about the person.

Ellen was glad Meg was enjoying herself, but she was getting fidgety. "We both don't need to do this, Meg. Why don't you keep going through the yearbooks, and I'll go to the church in Keaton?

If you find a picture of someone resembling the woman, just mark the page."

Meg was thoroughly engrossed in the yearbooks. "Take a look at this girl. Her name is Victoria Lake. She's the police chief's daughter." Meg pointed to a pretty girl with soft blond hair falling around her shoulders.

"That's not the woman we're looking for, if that's what you mean," said Ellen, pulling on her coat. "It's definitely not her."

"But this brings something back," said Meg, drumming her fingers on the table. "Yes, I remember. A while back, at a town picnic, I overheard a lady gossiping about the chief. She said that his wife was a beautiful woman who was so bored in this town that she began to go to bars for excitement, and the chief would go find her and practically drag her home. I also heard that he had met his wife at a police convention in Las Vegas, and it was one of those quick weddings."

Meg turned the page of the yearbook. "It's sort of romantic, when you think about it. At that time, he was a young hometown police officer, and the Las Vegas trip was probably the first time he'd been anywhere. He must have been completely dazzled when he met her. She may have been a showgirl, and of course she was probably dazzled by his blue uniform.

"And she must have seen a chance at a new life, in a sleepy little town," Meg continued. "The rumor is that one day she just left here and went back to Las Vegas. Then, after Victoria graduated, she rebelled against her father and went to live with her mother. Neither one of them ever came back to Springton."

Ellen's mind was on other things. She picked up her bag. "I think the chief is a very complicated man. Keep digging, Meg. Maybe you'll find something else."

Without looking up from the yearbook, Meg waved her away. "Well, maybe you'll be the one who finds some information today," she said, turning the page. "Good luck at that church in Keaton."

CHAPTER TWENTY-FOUR

Keaton, Massachusetts

Reverend Martin, the young pastor of the Community Church, greeted Ellen with a pleasant, easy manner. A solemn expression crossed his face when she told him that the purpose of her visit was to discuss her parents' bequest to the church.

"I wish I had known your parents personally," he said. "Mr. and Mrs. Von Der Hyde must have been very caring and giving people. It must please you to know that their gift lived on for so many years."

"What do you mean?" Ellen asked.

Looking puzzled, he said, "You understand that the money was designated to our church endowment fund."

"No, I don't understand. My parents didn't go to this church. Or any church, for that matter."

Pastor Martin nodded sympathetically. "I wasn't here at the time, of course, but I can tell you that this church was founded by wealthy families who set up endowments. The funds in some endowments were to be directed to specific institutions. One was the old monastery in Springton and that's where your parents directed their money. It's now called the Pomarium. That particular fund lasted for years and ran out before the monastery building was converted to a home for the aged."

"So my parents had their money funneled to the old monastery through the Community Church," Ellen said, almost to herself. "Why wouldn't they leave it directly to the monastery? Actually, why would they give them anything?"

The bells of the church began tolling, seeming to become louder with each peal. Pastor Martin was talking, but she barely heard his words. She was thinking of Meg, so worried about having enough money for her children's education, home improvements, and now taxes.

"As I was saying." The pastor's voice brought Ellen back into the present. "I hope your parents' bequest represented only a portion of the estate, and their survivors inherited a share, also."

"No, it's not like that at all," Ellen said softly.

"I see. I'm sorry it worked out that way. Is there anything else you'd like to ask?"

"Yes, one more thing, please. Now that the monastery has become a nursing home, would you know if any of the residents at the home were once monks there?"

"Why, yes. I made a pastoral visit to Brother Lester just last week. He's not always lucid, but if he's having a better day, maybe he can help you."

Ellen stood and shook the pastor's hand. "Thank you," she said. "I'll remember you."

"And I'll be praying for you and your family. I wish you well with your quest."

This is a quest, all right, thought Ellen, walking to the car. *A quest for the truth.*

She stopped at the first phone booth she saw and called Meg at the school to ask if she could keep the car a little longer. Meg said she could easily get someone to drive her home but wanted to know why. Ellen told her only that she was driving out to the Pomarium to talk to a resident named Brother Lester, and said a quick good-bye before Meg could ask another question.

CHAPTER TWENTY-FIVE

Ellen followed an aide through the halls of the Pomarium. She didn't remember ever being in this building when it was a monastery, but the vaulted ceilings and gothic windows made it easy to imagine lines of monks passing through the great halls on their way to prayers.

A rotund man with a head full of snowy white hair sat in a wheelchair in the day room. A brightly colored afghan covered him up to his shoulders. He was staring into a fireplace that held no fire.

"It's not one of Brother Lester's good days," the aide whispered. "But you can try."

An elderly woman, her auburn hair speckled with gray, came over to them and set a glass of orange juice on the table next to his chair. She touched his hand gently. "Brother Lester, here's some orange juice, your favorite. And you have a visitor today."

The woman pulled a chair close to Ellen. "You'll have to speak up, dear," she said, then turned and picked up a stack of empty trays from a nearby table.

Ellen thanked the woman, then sat. "Brother Lester, my name

is Ellen," she said. "I've come to ask if you remember my brother, Eric Von Der Hyde."

At the loud gasp behind her, Ellen turned. The woman who had been serving the juice stared at Ellen with an expression of disbelief. Then, trays in hand, she hurried out of the day room.

Ellen glanced at Brother Lester, whose eyes were closed. She gave the aide a questioning look.

The aide shrugged. "It doesn't look like he'll be able to help you today. I'm sorry."

What had Pastor Martin said? *Quest*, Ellen thought. *I'm not giving up yet.* She thanked the aide and hurried to catch up with the auburn-haired woman, who had rushed out a side door. She was nowhere in sight.

Following a cobblestone walk which took her behind the main structure to a smaller building, Ellen remembered Julian describing how the monks walked there for their meals. She guessed that this building was now being used for the main kitchen. Curls of smoke rose from the chimney, and she could smell pleasant cooking aromas.

When she peered through the window pane of the wooden door, she saw the woman who had been serving the juice. She was stirring a long wooden spoon in a pot on the cast iron stove, which was as huge as Julian had described. Ellen's tap on the window caused the woman to turn. Nodding her head to Ellen, as if she were expecting her, the woman put down the spoon and opened the door.

Ellen stepped into the kitchen, enjoying its warmth and the smell of what might be beef stew. The assorted pots and pans hung on hooks above a wooden countertop that ran the length of the room.

When she began to introduce herself, the woman interrupted by holding up a hand. In an Irish brogue, she said, "I already heard you say your name. I should have known before you spoke. You look just like him. Please, have a seat." She pointed to a wooden chair painted green and then put two cups and saucers on the table. From the stove, she brought a restaurant-sized kettle from which she poured two cups of steaming water. Ellen's heart was racing. This woman knew Eric.

The woman placed a tea bag in each cup. She sat across from Ellen and said, "It's in the eyes. Not so much the color, but the light. I know there's no putting off the likes of you. You'll only come back. Like he did."

Ellen eased the tea bag out of the cup and put it on the saucer, then helped herself to sugar from a cracked bowl and stirred the tea. "Thank you so much for letting me in," she said. "What's your name?"

The woman seemed pleased by the question. "My name is about all I have left from the homeland," she said, picking up a china creamer and passing it to Ellen. "It's Rosemary Flanagan. But I'm called Rose."

The woman was thin yet big-boned, with capable hands that covered her tea cup when she lifted it to her lips. The net cap holding her hair highlighted the profile of her face, which Ellen thought was very pretty.

A strong and kind and compassionate face, Ellen thought.

"Tell me why you've come here," said Rose.

Ellen took a breath. "My brother died very recently. He worked here many years ago, and I'm trying to find someone who remembers him."

Rose lowered her tea cup to the saucer, spilling some of the contents on the tablecloth. "Eric Von Der Hyde dead? Oh, no." She twisted the hem of her apron nervously. "Then that means she's not with him. Oh dear, this can't be."

Rose used the hem of her apron to rub at the tea stain. "If she's not with him, then, where is she?"

"Where is who?" Ellen asked.

As if talking to herself, Rose said, "When she left the way she did, I was sure it was because he sent for her. But if he's dead, then where can she be? Oh, glory be, let Theresa be safe."

"Rose, tell me. Please. Who is Theresa?"

Rose was looking beyond Ellen, as if she were gazing into the past.

The woman's genuine sadness touched Ellen, and she patted Rose's wrist. "You don't know me, Rose, but you knew my brother, and you can trust me. I may be able to help you. That's why I'm here. To find a woman who may have had a connection to Eric. From what you are saying, it could very well be Theresa. May I tell you what is happening and what I've learned so far?"

Rose dabbed her eyes with her apron and nodded. "Yes, go on."

It was getting late in the afternoon, and Ellen decided to keep strictly to the facts surrounding Eric's death.

She explained that Eric left instructions for Julian Baker to handle the arrangements, that his sisters didn't know the reason for the secrecy. She described the mystery woman who visited the family gravesite. Rose listened quietly, moving only to cross herself when Ellen mentioned the woman.

"It's definitely Theresa. Thank heavens she's been seen. She disappeared last Thursday. I don't know why she hasn't come back to work."

Rose went over to the stove and came back with more steaming hot water, then repeated the tea making process with fresh tea bags. Laying out slices of brown bread and a crock of butter, she put a plate and knife in front of Ellen. Ellen didn't feel like eating, but politely spread butter on a slice of bread.

Sitting back in her chair, Rose said, "Maybe it will help a little if I tell you my story. I came from Ireland when I was eighteen to live here, in the little house next door, with my aunt. She was head cook here, you see, and I was hired as a helper. When she died some years later, I took her job. Then—maybe twenty-five years ago—they hired on a girl for the summer, to help me in the kitchen. That was Theresa. She was nearly seventeen when she started here, but oh, what a lonely child she was. My heart just broke for her. It was so hard to know what she was thinking. She didn't talk much, and I gathered she had no friends. And she never mentioned her home. I got the feeling something bad had happened there.

"That summer, the monastery also hired a young man to work in the orchards. He was as polite as he was strong, never asked for a thing. One scorching day in July, I put up a tray of lemonade and sent Theresa out to the orchards to bring it to him." Rose smiled at the memory. "Oh, did she protest, that girl was so shy. When she saw him coming closer to the border of the orchard, right over there, near the wall, she turned around and ran back here, tray and all."

Ellen turned and followed Rose's gaze to the window to the stone wall, about two feet high, that Julian had pointed out to her.

"He helped build that wall, too," Rose added.

"I know," murmured Ellen. It was all she knew about Eric up to now, she thought sadly, and even that had to come from Julian.

Rose continued. "I said, 'Glory, girl, he's not going to bite you. As strong as he is, that boy will faint away in this sun without any nourishment.' One day, she finally got enough courage to bring him the tray, and I can see it now. Her staring down to the ground when he turned to look at her, his smile when he saw the pitcher of lemonade.

"She was so embarrassed, she ran back in here again. He was nice enough to return the tray, the pitcher, and the glass, right here in this kitchen. He was so polite. He thanked both of us, all the while smiling at Theresa. And after that, Theresa made up the trays herself and each afternoon, she brought him a cold drink and even cookies that she put aside just for him.

"And every time she did this they would talk longer and longer, and sometimes they went off together, happy as could be, into the orchard."

Leaning closer to Ellen and lowering her voice to a whisper, Rose said, "They had to go far into the orchard to talk, you see, because their laughter carried over to the main house, and the monks had strict rules about quiet. I couldn't believe the change in the girl. I had not seen her laugh until then. She became radiant, and all her beauty began to show. He brought it out in her, you see."

Rose fell silent.

"Please go on," Ellen said gently. "It's all right. He was my brother."

Rose continued in a whisper. "Well, sometime that fall, your brother stopped coming here. What I heard was that your parents sent him away to a military school. Nearly broke Theresa's heart, but she kept up her work, coming in to help me out on weekends and a few days during the week, after school.

"One morning I was in the kitchen, just before dawn. I heard a car door open and then close and sounds of tires screeching. I thought I heard a kitten mewing. Thinking someone had dropped off a stray, I opened the door and who was it but Theresa, whimpering in a huddle with only a paper bag with her things in it. I brought her in and gave her a cup of tea, and we sat here like you and I are doing right now."

Ellen shivered even though the radiator was steaming and heat came from pots on the stove. "Do you remember what month it was?" she asked.

November, I think it was, before Thanksgiving. Theresa was wearing her school uniform. She couldn't have been more than seventeen. The girl cried her heart out right at this kitchen table, sitting where you are now.

"After I got Theresa calmed down, she helped me peel apples for the pies. Later that morning, I was told by the people here that Theresa Francis would be working and residing here for good."

"Theresa Francis," Ellen repeated, grateful to finally have the woman's first and last name.

Rose nodded. "There was enough room in the little house for two. My aunt and I had lived here together, after all. But it was a shame. I was an adult, and it was my choice to be there. But with Theresa, it was a different story. She wanted to be in school. But she didn't have a say in the matter. She never said, but I just knew her family didn't want her." In a whisper, Rose added, "She was in the family way, you see."

"And Eric was the father," said Ellen. She didn't feel surprised. It simply felt as if a piece of the puzzle had fallen into place.

"That's right. But no one was to know about the baby, not even him. Why, Eric wouldn't have gone off just like that if he knew she was pregnant. I'm sure of that."

"What happened to the baby?"

Rose's eyes filled again. "The baby. Theresa was so sad at first, but then whenever she felt the new life inside her, she became happy. She said it wouldn't be good for the baby if its mother was sad all the time.

"And, oh, the work we got done in this kitchen. I didn't let her do anything heavy, like lifting pots, of course. It all came together for her. She loved to make fruit pies. Why, the monks wouldn't have had any fruit left over for their jelly if it had been up to Theresa. She was real smart, too smart to be in a kitchen all the time. She learned Latin by herself, and she'd hum the chants. Theresa was a blessing, and I was so thankful every day for that girl, and then, and then—." Rose stopped talking and began tracing the threads on the tablecloth again.

"The baby came?" Ellen guessed.

"Oh, poor little baby, poor Theresa. I will only tell you that she had a rough time delivering, and when the choice had to be made between the mother and the baby, they saved the mother."

Rose bowed her head and then continued. "It was a cold March night, and when the pains began, they took her to Doctor

Sutton up on the hill. That was all pre-arranged, I knew that much.

"I guessed that whoever her family was, they didn't want Theresa to give birth in the hospital because of the disgrace once the town people found out. I wondered what kind of family they were, but I never asked questions. You get like the monks when you've been here this long. You keep things to yourself."

Looking at the clock on the wall, Rose got to her feet. "I shouldn't say this, but I think I've figured out who her family was, and if Theresa doesn't come back tomorrow, I'll tell you. Right now, that girl is following her heart, just like she did so many years ago, and I need to leave her be and not be putting myself into her private business."

Ellen remembered the card Theresa had left at the grave with the baby's name. She patted Rose's hand. "If she never told you, I want you to know that Theresa's baby was a girl, and she gave her the beautiful name of Rose.

After you."

CHAPTER TWENTY-SIX

Orchard Road was the only direct route back to town from the old monastery, and Ellen drove slowly, mindful of the nails that had flattened Meg's tires. She was on her way to visit Julian, ignoring his request that she call first. She had more questions for him than asking to read Eric's letter. Julian seemed to be the type to plan things in orderly fashion. A surprise visit might throw him off and work in her favor.

At the end of the road, Ellen took a left turn on Main Street and noticed a Chevrolet Bel Air idling on the side of the road. The driver pulled out behind her, flicking his headlamps. She drove two blocks and pulled into the first public parking place she saw, in front of Patty's Diner. The driver of the Bel Air passed her by a car's length, stopped with a screech of brakes, and backed into the space in front of hers. Ellen was already out of the car and had reached the top step of the diner when a familiar voice—one she never wanted to hear again—stopped her cold.

The voice of her ex-husband.

"Hey, Ellen. It's me, Billy."

Turning, she said, angrily, "You! What a nerve, following me. I haven't seen you since the divorce. That's not long enough for me."

"I know, I know," he said, taking the steps and standing in front of her. "But this is important."

"Why? Have you put my name on another loan?"

She took in his square jaw and short-cropped hair. To her astonishment, she could now place Marty Smith, the man she had watched from the restaurant window as he was being led out in handcuffs. Billy's resemblance to his cousin Marty was startling. She might have realized it before if she hadn't blocked Billy out of her mind so completely.

"I promise, this is legitimate," he was saying. "I figured Meg wouldn't want me at the house, and I remembered where Carl's shop was, so I went there. He told me you'd be coming out at the intersection of Main and Orchard. Carl's okay with this, Ellen. He even described Meg's car so I wouldn't miss you. Can we go in for a cup of coffee so I can tell you why I'm here?"

Ellen gave a reluctant nod, and let Billy push open the door to the diner for her.

Ellen stepped inside, then turned to face him. "I know why you're here. You have a cousin, Marty Smith. You introduced us once, a long time ago, and last week I watched him get arrested. So this has something to do with my counterfeiting-ring story, right?"

A worried look crossed Billy's face. "Right."

In a booth by the window, Billy lit a cigarette, inhaled deeply, and blew the smoke away from Ellen. "You know, you were always very pretty, but now you're beautiful."

"I don't want to hear that from you. Just get to the point."

He pointed to the jukebox on the table. "For old times' sake, would you like to hear one of our sentimental songs?"

"Stop it. This isn't exactly a sentimental visit," Ellen said, nodding a thank you to a waitress who set two glasses of water on the table. She gripped the glass with both hands, keeping her eyes straight on him. "Just start at the beginning."

Billy smiled, exposing nicotine-stained teeth. "Well, if you hadn't taken back your maiden name, maybe none of this would be happening. Ellen Smith is a bit more anonymous then Ellen Von Der Hyde, wouldn't you think? I'm referring to your big story with your byline on the front page."

"I don't have a single regret about taking back my maiden name. And I didn't know that Marty was part of the counterfeiting ring. Besides, I don't think it would have mattered."

Billy crushed his half-smoked cigarette in a glass ashtray. "Okay, let's get to it. Marty was in jail only for a couple of hours the day of the sting. He had his own connections. When he read your story, he was determined to find out the name of your informant. He began to follow you."

"Was he planning to hurt me?"

"No, not Marty. He just wanted to intimidate you enough to name the snitch."

Ellen thought back to the incidents of the last few days. "Like making it look he was running a car off the road? Or putting nails in the tires?"

With a frown, Billy said, "Putting a scare into you on the road, yes. Nails in the tires, no. Maybe breaking into your apartment and rummaging through your things, stuff like that."

Oh, my God, the Nowaks, thought Ellen, then, with relief, remembered they were away. "How did you know I was here, in Springton?"

"I read your story, so I knew where you worked. I called the newspaper."

Ellen set the water glass down and leaned back in the booth, wanting to put distance between them. "I can't believe anyone at the paper told you where I was."

"No one did. The telephone operator said you were on funeral leave, and I knew your family lived here. I'm sorry your brother died. Carl told me at least that much. I know how your sister feels about me."

That's right, Ellen thought. *Your name is never mentioned.* "I don't want to talk about my family with you. Marty is why you're here. I'm going to report him to the police."

"You won't have to. That's the other reason why I'm here. To tell you that Marty was found dead early this morning, in Boston Harbor. It's being called a drowning accident, but no one believes that. I'm guessing the word got out that Marty was looking for your informant."

"I'm sorry about your cousin," Ellen said. It wasn't that she had much sympathy for Marty, but the thought of him being drowned in icy Boston Harbor shook her. He might have been a crook and a creep, but no one deserved that.

Ellen wondered what else Billy knew. She didn't want to believe that Jake would murder anyone, but he would have connections no matter where he went. Word on the street traveled fast. She was reminded of Jake's last words to her: 'Make sure somebody's got your back, lady. Like you had mine'.

The waitress came to the table with her pad and pencil. Ellen shook her head. Billy ordered a BLT.

Ellen reached for her bag. "Why would you come here to warn me about a dead man? He can't scare anyone now."

Billy shrugged. "I figured you should know the kind of people you're dealing with. Marty was into counterfeiting and other big-league stuff. Your snitch took a real chance by talking to you." He shrugged, then said, "As for me, I'm small potatoes. I just play cards." At her dark look, he said, "All right, I just wanted to warn you to be careful in the city. There's lots of bad guys like Marty out there."

Ellen had no idea what she was going to do about any of that. Her mind was already on what she would say to Julian. "Okay, thanks and good-bye," she said, getting to her feet.

Billy gestured with a wave of his hand. "But you're real safe in this little town."

I hope you're right about that, thought Ellen, not looking back as she hurried to the door.

CHAPTER TWENTY-SEVEN

Two elderly women, their arms linked together, walked solemnly down the front stairs of the Baker Funeral Home. They nodded in unison to Ellen, as if expressing mutual sympathy, and she nodded in return.

After her unsettling meeting with Billy, which she was trying to put out of her mind for now, Ellen continued with her plan of confronting Julian and demanding that he let her see Eric's instructions for herself.

She was sure that Julian wouldn't appreciate her unscheduled visit any more than she had appreciated Billy's. She put her hand on a huge doorknob and almost stumbled across the threshold when the door swung open.

An unsmiling Julian stood in front of her. "It's not that I was waiting here to greet you, Ellen," he said in a low tone. "I was just seeing those people out the door." He looked her up and down, then said, "We'll talk in my office." He led her through a large foyer, away from a room where mourners were gathered, and down a long hallway. The walls were filled with landscape paintings.

Ellen knew just enough about art to recognize that the paintings were of high quality.

"You seem to be quite taken with my collection," Julian said, leading her past a room with a casket surrounded by baskets of flowers. "I have a few more, too good for public viewing, at least to me."

Ellen didn't know what that comment meant and decided to let it slide.

Taking a key ring from his pocket, Julian unlocked a door into a spacious office furnished with mahogany bookshelves, tables, a desk and leather chairs. He held out a chair for her and walked behind his desk. Pushing a button on the telephone, he requested that no calls be taken, then sat, staring at Ellen.

"I have the sense that you were expecting me, Julian." Ellen spoke in deliberate, calm tones, trying to hide her rising anxiety. She had to stay in control. The drive from the high school to the church in Keaton, then to the Pomarium, with all its revelations, and now back full circle, to the center of town, had taken its toll. To say nothing of Billy Smith appearing back in her life with news that rattled her.

Julian nodded, a smug expression on his face. "Ever since you got back to Springton, I've been keeping my eye on you, looking out for you, the way Eric would have wanted me to."

"Don't," Ellen said, the very idea making her stomach churn. "You're not Eric and I don't need you to look out for me."

Julian shrugged. "Nevertheless, when I heard you were going to the Pomarium, to talk to an old monk, I figured you'd stop here on your way back. After all, this is the end of the line, isn't it? In more ways than one, I might add."

"If you know where I went today, you've obviously talked to Meg."

Seeming pleased that he knew something she didn't, he said, "Of course. I drove her home from the library."

Ellen stifled a sigh. *Oh, Meg,* she thought. *Why do you tell Julian all our business? Don't you realize he hasn't offered a scrap of information to help us?*

She leaned forward. "You had calling hours today. How did you find time to pick up Meg?"

"I have a staff," he said, pride showing on his face. "Triple the size my father had."

"Julian, you said you would show me Eric's letter. That's one of the reasons why I'm here."

"You know, funny thing. I looked this morning, and sorry to say, I can't put my finger on it. I'll let you know as soon as it turns up." He stood. She was dismissed.

Ellen remained seated. "I said that's *one* of the reasons I'm here. I'm also looking for information about a baby that Eric fathered. With Theresa Francis."

Julian's lips formed a thin line. "That's preposterous," he said. "That monk must have been really out of it if he told you a story like that. I've never heard of a Theresa Francis." He let out a hollow laugh. "You wasted your time going out to that old place."

"On the contrary, it was a good use of my time. I met a woman by the name of Rose, and I feel as if I'm finally getting someplace."

Julian blinked. "Yes, I remember Rose, from when Eric worked there. She's visited here a number of times for funerals since then. As you may imagine, this is the final destination for many of the residents of the Pomarium. Well," he asked, his eyes narrowing, "what did Rose tell you?"

"That the infant, a baby girl, died at birth."

"That's all you have? I know firsthand how good you are at asking questions. She must have told you something more than that."

"Well, she didn't, and besides, that's her business, not mine, and certainly not yours. I have reason to think that the baby may be buried in my family's plot."

"You can't be serious."

"I'm more than serious, Julian."

"You like digging around so much, maybe you can take a shovel and find out for yourself."

Ignoring his sarcasm, Ellen said, "You're not making this easy for either one of us. Just show me whatever files you have."

"As if I don't have anything better to do with my time."

She leaned in, closer to the desk. "You found time to pick up Meg today."

"You seem to have answers for everything, Ellen."

"If I had all the answers, the last place I would spend my time is in a funeral home, talking to you."

With an annoyed glance at her, he picked up the phone and asked his receptionist for the Von Der Hyde file. She came in within minutes and placed it on his desk.

"The file is still out because of Eric's recent funeral," Julian said. "No other reason, in case that suspicious mind of yours is wondering."

Without opening it, he pushed the folder across the desktop. Ellen could tell by his actions there would be nothing there. She quickly scanned the pages, which included a copy of the deed to the family plot and a diagram. There were six sections in the plot, three of them filled. Rudolph, Esther, and Eric Von Der Hyde. Her family.

"I trust you're satisfied," Julian said. "Now you can believe me when I say that I don't know any more than you do." He came around the desk and opened the office door. "Good-bye, Ellen."

Ellen didn't make a move to get up. Slowly, she said, "Theresa's baby was born about a quarter of a century ago. Your father was the only undertaker in town at that time, so he most likely handled the burial. I'd like you to check that out in his old files."

Julian shook his head. "Maybe tomorrow. But be sure to call first."

"Tomorrow won't do. I'm going back to Boston. We need to do this right now."

His face darkening, he said, "I don't have time to argue, so be my guest, and follow me. That is, if you don't mind dank and stuffy cellars."

Ellen followed him down a set of back stairs and into a musty cellar. To the left of the landing was a wall with several locked doors. A sign on the first door read "Toxic Materials." The wall on her right had no doors.

Julian walked to the end and took a right, into a section that ran the length of the basement. It was stacked with crates and cartons which formed a partition in the center of the floor. On the other side was an arrangement of old furniture, very much like Harvey's, set up like an office. "This is my father's stuff. Everything is still in the desk drawers and file cabinets. Someday I'll go through this mess that he left me."

Julian stooped to open the bottom drawer of a rusted-out file cabinet and flipped through the indexes. "No names that begin with a V," he said lightly. "Sorry."

Standing next to him while he closed the drawer, she said, "Now open the second drawer and find the last name Francis. Infant Rose Francis."

Julian straightened and turned, a puzzled look on his face. A cobweb swayed over his head. He reached up and angrily brushed it away. Ellen heard a faint scurrying from within the wall.

"You're really serious, aren't you?" he said. "Look, I don't care if you want to waste your time, but when it comes to squandering mine, you are way out of line."

He pulled a folder from the drawer and thrust it at her. "The Francis family, beginning in 1900. Take your time," he said, pulling out a dusty swivel chair. "Come upstairs when you're finished and I'll let you out." He turned and walked away, leaving her alone in the makeshift office that had a chemical smell to it. The noises behind the walls seemed to be getting closer, and she couldn't help thinking of the departed souls in the viewing rooms upstairs.

After a few minutes, Ellen slammed the folder shut, causing

particles of dust to stream upwards, making her sneeze. She was furious with Julian for leaving her alone in this crypt-like basement and it didn't help any that he was right. Over a span of three generations, there was no record of a death of anyone in the Francis family under the age of twenty. Their family members died mostly of old age and natural causes, or, as in the case of a twenty-year-old, by a farm accident.

As she returned the file to the drawer, Ellen heard the same scurrying she had heard earlier. Turning her head quickly, she saw a mouse running around the inside of a carton made limp by the dampness of the cellar. Appearing to be as startled as Ellen, it stopped and looked at her, then began chasing around the carton again.

We have something in common, little mouse, she thought. *We're both scurrying around in a maze, but let me tell you, I will find my way out.* She closed the drawer and then noticed the silence. The mouse was gone.

Still furious with Julian, she walked up the stairs and let herself out the front door. When she turned the ignition on Meg's car, she was sure he was watching, but she wouldn't give him the satisfaction of looking up.

CHAPTER TWENTY-EIGHT

Sunday, March 13

Wendell was driving home after a few Sunday deliveries and turning the radio knob to find his favorite mystery show. A jingle for geriatric medicine blared through the staticky radio, triggering a thought that made him jam on the brakes. He had forgotten to deliver a carton of medical supplies to the Pomarium. Mr. Chadwick, the town pharmacist, always paid him well. He didn't want to make him angry.

Wendell turned around and drove out to the Pomarium, parked the van, and when he reached for the carton, saw a basket that he hadn't noticed earlier. He had no idea how it had gotten there. The basket was wrapped in cellophane and tied with a gold ribbon. An envelope with his name on it was taped to the handle of the basket. When he opened the envelope, a ten-dollar bill fell out. Wendell stuffed it in his pocket, then read the note. There were hand-printed instructions to deliver the basket to Rose Flanagan. It was a surprise gift, so he was to leave it on the front step without ringing the doorbell.

The nice Irish cook always asked him how he was, and sometimes gave him samples of the food she was cooking. Not like that

Theresa, who never spoke to him unless he spoke first, and sometimes not even then. He wondered if he would have had a chance with Theresa if she hadn't met that Von Der Hyde boy first.

It must have been because Eric was good-looking, and he was all pimply faced. Well, it doesn't matter now, he thought. Eric was dead and Theresa was gone.

But he was still here. And he was going to make sure Rose got that basket. All the better, he thought, because it would be dark out, and she wouldn't see him deliver the surprise.

In the three days since Theresa went away, Rose finally felt some peace. Her talk with Ellen Von Der Hyde gave her hope about Theresa. Rose was sure the poor girl was in shock. After all, the only love of her life was never coming back, and he had promised her he would.

It had been years since Rose had thought about who Theresa's parents may have been. She had her suspicions, which she kept to herself. It might make more trouble for Theresa, and she couldn't bear that.

But if Theresa didn't come back soon, it would be only right that Rose share her suspicions with someone. They had to search for her sometime, and the only person she would trust would be Eric's sister. This time they would talk right here, in the home that she and Theresa shared, and she would name the family that she thought Theresa came from. Maybe as early as tomorrow.

Rose sat in her favorite chair, an overstuffed one that had belonged to her aunt, with her feet resting on the matching hassock. She had talked the director of the Pomarium into not replacing Theresa right away, so for these last few days, Rose's working hours had been longer, and her legs were feeling the strain.

But she wouldn't have it any other way. No one in the world could replace Theresa Francis.

Instead of turning on the television, her nightly routine, Rose reflected on the surprise gift she had found on her doorstep just an hour earlier.

It was nighttime when she had come around to the front door, and there was just enough of a glow from the outdoor lamp for her to see the basket on the top step.

Tucked inside the basket was a plain gift card with no signature, just a printed message reading, *With Sincere Thanks.* Rose couldn't think of anyone who would be sending her such a gift. Maybe it was from Ellen Von Der Hyde, her way of showing appreciation for their talk.

The basket contained tins of crackers and a box of tea bags. Tucked in the middle of the basket was a jar of jelly the color of peaches, reminding Rose of happier times. There was no label, so she imagined it was a delicacy made from someone in town.

Rose hadn't been very hungry when she came upstairs, so the items in the basket made a perfect light supper. She had spread the peach jelly over a few crackers and put them on a china plate with little shamrocks hand-painted on the rim. Then she stirred the tea into a cup that matched the plate.

She was as efficient in her own little kitchen as she was in the huge monastery kitchen. Before sitting at her table, she had put away the jar of jelly in the refrigerator and stored the crackers and tea in the cupboard, then taken bites of the crackers in between sips of tea, savoring the way one taste complemented the other. She had washed and dried the plate and cup and put them in the china closet that had also belonged to her aunt, before going into the living room and easing herself into her chair.

With a hand-knitted shawl wrapped around her shoulders, she welcomed the peaceful drowsiness that settled in like warm dusk on a summer evening, giving herself over to the pleasant memories triggered by the taste and aroma of the peach jelly.

Her gentle wave of nostalgia suddenly turned into a crushing wave of nausea as a cramping pain streaked through her abdomen, then crisscrossed across her chest, turning everything in her line of vision into a grid of purple and black, like a hurricane slamming into an orchard, bruising and destroying everything in its path.

CHAPTER TWENTY-NINE

Monday, March 14

Ellen spent most of Monday at the Springton Library doing one of the things she was best at—research. She went through hours of microfilm, looking for anything she could find on Theresa Francis. But there was nothing. She made equally poor progress with Theresa's baby. There was no birth announcement and no obituary. Everything about Theresa Francis seemed shrouded in secrecy.

It was late afternoon when Ellen finished at the library. She had also searched for information on the monastery and on Julian, wondering if she would find anything to explain her own misgivings. But all she found connected to Julian were write-ups about how he made his father's business more successful and how he someday hoped to run for a position on the town council. Finally, she searched the Boston papers for more information on Jake the jockey. There were a few stories connected to his run-ins with the law and Boston's criminal underground.

By the time she boarded the early evening train back to Boston, she had learned that Julian was more of a prominent citizen than she'd thought, Jake far more dangerous than she'd guessed, and Theresa was as much of a mystery as she had been the day of Eric's funeral.

Ellen dialed Nick's number the minute she walked into her apartment. Although she had no right to expect him to be waiting at the train station, she had been disappointed when he wasn't there. *Why should he put himself out*, she thought, *after the way I treated him at Meg's house?*

"Hello, Nick," she said when he answered.

After a pause, he said. "So, Madame Editor, I take it you're back."

She took a deep breath. "Look. I know I may have come across as being rude to you."

"'May have'?"

He wasn't going to make this easy. "All right, Nick. I admit I wasn't at my best. And I'm sorry about that. Let's talk about the presentation. How did it go?"

"Well, I wouldn't say the word 'go' is appropriate. Let's just say that it went."

Clutching the phone, she said, "What do you mean, 'it went'? What happened?"

"'What happened'?" he exploded. "First of all, you stick me with this on a weekend, assuring me that the presentation, due Monday, is all prepared."

She kept her voice cool. "I wouldn't say the word 'stick' is appropriate."

"What you neglected to tell me was that 'all prepared' meant everything was still in Brenda's files and, since she took Monday off, I was up a creek without a paddle. Let me correct that. We're in the city now. Let's say that I was on Fifth Avenue without any clothes."

Trying not to form a visual image of that, she said, "I don't understand. I gave it to Brenda on Thursday before I left for Springton, with instructions to type it up immediately. She never allows a backlog."

"What's the expression? Something about when the mouse is away?"

"Nick, get to the point. The presentation. Did it or did it not take place?"

"Oh, it took place all right. After I spent most of the day piecing together the work Brenda had actually done on it, which I would say was about twenty-five percent, I managed to put the remaining seventy-five percent together. Once I found the information, of course."

"But how was the presentation?"

"You get an A for content," he said. "The entire proposal was accepted. Even the budget. But I didn't appreciate doing the clerical work. If you did this because I didn't do the story you wanted, then touché."

"That remark was uncalled for," she said angrily. "You should know me better that that."

It was his turn to take a deep breath. "You caught me at the wrong time. I just got in. I guess I do know you better that that." There was a silence.

Ellen fingered the telephone, making little ringlets with the cord, then let the coils spring. "I was wondering," she said, "if you would like to come over. There's a leftover slice of apple pie here."

"I really don't feel like having dessert right now."

Her heart sank, then lightened, when he asked, "How about if I bring Chinese food? Then we can argue over the last slice of pie?"

"Only if you hurry. I'm starved," she said with relief.

They ate fried rice and chicken wings out of containers on the kitchen table and drank white wine. Nick smiled while he watched her nibble on the last chicken wing. "And just what are you smiling at?" she asked.

"I was just thinking I'm glad you're back, even if you did stick it to me."

"That's not fair, Nick. The problem lies with Brenda, and there's not a thing I can do until tomorrow. Everyone knows she's been under a lot of pressure at home, with her mother being so sick. She's been trying to get her into a nursing home."

Nick didn't seem impressed. "Not only was she careless, but she couldn't have cared less. I called her, and she didn't call me back. Besides, you won't believe a mistake she made—."

"Look," Ellen said, interrupting him. "I apologize for putting you on the spot that way, though it was never my intention. I just got caught up in things in Springton."

"I was going to ask you about that," Nick said. "If you recall, when we last parted, the heroine was going to continue the search for the stranger wearing the red scarf. But first, at the suggestion of her good friend who happens to be her subordinate professional, she was going to provide some information so he could help her sort out some of the pieces of the events of what may or may not have contributed to the death of the police chief. That conversation, you see, was to have taken place on their drive back to Boston, but, alas, the good friend was dumped. Like a bag of peanut shells."

Ellen looked away and smiled, trying not to reveal how good it felt to be with him again. "I'd rather bring you up to date another time," she said. "I'm saturated with it all right now."

They walked into the living room with their wine glasses and sat on the floor.

"Okay, change of subject. This is where you belong," Nick said, gesturing with his free hand. "Right here, in this apartment, in this city. You were like a fish out of water at your sister's house. Every time you tried to do something in the kitchen, Meg got a stricken look on her face. Did you ever ask yourself why she's always suggesting that you relax in the living room with a cup of coffee?"

"Now that you mention it, yes." Ellen laughed, thinking of Meg grabbing the dish she was going to use for butter. "I guess I am something like a bull in a china shop. Poor Meg."

Nick hit the side of his head with his hand. "I forgot to tell you something. One of the counterfeiters who was arrested was only jailed for a few hours. The guy would have been safer if he stayed in jail. He was fished out of Boston Harbor. His name was Marty Smith."

"I wanted to tell you that, too," said Ellen. At Nick's inquisitive look, she said, "I didn't know it at the time, but Marty Smith was my ex-husband's cousin. My ex came to Springton to tell me Marty was dead. It's also possible that it was Marty who tried to scare us off the road on our way to Springton. Apparently, he was thinking that if I got scared enough, I'd give up Jake's name."

"Sounds to me like your ex has your back," said Nick.

"That was the end of it," Ellen said adamantly. "He knows I never want to see him again."

"I will be more than happy to drink to that," said Nick, raising his glass and downing the wine.

When they said good night at the door, Nick put his arms around her and drew her close. "Let's talk more about the mystery in your hometown tomorrow," he said.

Her knees felt shaky. She wanted him to hold her longer, but he released his arms and said, before he headed down the stairs, "Italian take-out, okay?"

She could only nod because the words wouldn't come.

Relieved and happy to be in her own bed, Ellen fell asleep right away. The familiar traffic noises were soothing to her but faded away when the dream started again. The man appeared at her bedroom doorway and then stepped back. She bolted up, terrified, and turned on the bed lamp.

Her lighted bedroom was not the cramped room of her childhood, with a drapery for a makeshift door. This bedroom had a door with hinges. Instead of chirping crickets from outside, there were blaring traffic sounds.

And there was no one standing in her doorway. With hands that were shaking, Ellen reached for her phone and dialed Nick's number. He picked up after one ring.

Taking short breaths, she gasped, "If you're serious about helping me fit the pieces to the puzzle, come over, Nick. I just woke up from a dream, but I think it's real. I'm afraid I won't remember everything in the morning. Can you come?"

"I'm on my way," he said, and hung up.

Ellen checked the time on her clock radio. It was one-thirty. How would she and Nick ever go into the office in just a few hours? They would both be half-asleep. Still, she needed to do this. She went over each detail of the dream over and over, writing down as much of it as she could. She never remembered dreams, but this was a nightmare. And she'd had it before.

Nick seemed to arrive in minutes. She had thrown an over-sized sweatshirt over her short pajamas and tied her hair back with a green ribbon. Ellen opened the door and grabbed his arm when he came in.

"Please sit down," she said, pointing to the sofa. She sat with her back to the arm of the couch, her feet tucked under her. He sat on the other side, facing her.

Nick was quiet for a moment after she described her dream. Then he said, "You realize this was no dream. It's a memory."

She nodded. "I know. But I can't remember all of what happened. Please ask me some questions. I think I can remember waking up in my parents' bed."

"The man. Try to picture him. Who was he?"

Ellen shook her head in frustration. "It isn't clear to me. His face was in the shadows upstairs, and downstairs, his back was to me."

"But it had something to do with Eric. What?"

"It must have had something to do with his being sent away to military prep school. I'm pretty sure this happened just before that. But I was only eight. I would have only asked where Eric was, not the reasons behind it."

"You know, maybe this fits in with what's going on in your hometown, and your subconscious is trying to surface, to bring something back."

Her voice breaking, Ellen said, "I can believe that, but I just don't know what it is." She put her head down, wanting to roll herself into a ball, just like she did that night. She again felt pressure of arms holding her, protecting her. Only these arms were stronger. Nick held her tenderly, his mouth pressed to her ear.

"I've never felt like this about anyone," he whispered. "I mean it." He kissed her from her earlobe to her neck, then tilted her chin lightly with his finger so that she was facing him. Ellen put her arms around him, under his shirt, and could feel the ripples from the muscles in his back. She thought she would die if he didn't kiss her on the mouth. When he did, she returned his kiss. The sound of a distant train brought her back, reminding her of that night many years ago. Nick lifted her sweatshirt, and she pulled away. In between quick breaths, she said, "I want to, but I can't. Not right now."

Nick stood and put the tail of his shirt in his pants. Looking like he was in pain, he swallowed hard and said, "Maybe we were both caught up in the moment. I'm not going to take back what I said, but I need time to think." He forced a smile. "I'll think about it, that is, while I take a cold shower when I get home."

She smiled. "That makes two of us."

He went to the door. "About tomorrow night. Italian food it is, but I think it would be best if we eat at a restaurant. Not here." He rubbed her cheek with the back of his hand. "No more dreams for tonight. You're making me crazy."

Ellen went back to bed and fell into a dreamy sleep. In her dream, Nick was holding her, and everything was all right again.

CHAPTER THIRTY

Tuesday, March 15

Even though she was desperate for another hour of sleep, Ellen forced herself out of bed at six a.m. She took a quick shower and put on the first outfit she pulled out of her closet: a tan jacket, a white blouse, and a black skirt that fell an inch beneath her knee. Glancing at her frumpy image in the mirror, she thought, *I've never threaded a needle in my life. Maybe Meg will hem this skirt for me.* She put on her low-heeled shoes that made it easy for walking, grabbed her bag, and rushed out the door. It wasn't until she got out to the street that she realized she had put no thought into wearing a dressier outfit for dinner with Nick.

Her mind was on her eight o'clock meeting with Sylvia Cummings, the personnel manager, about Brenda.

One hour later, Ellen sat in Sylvia's office. Sylvia had worked for several companies in Boston and was well known by a lot of insiders. She was seventy years old but kept putting retirement off. She got right to the point.

"I heard something very troubling about Brenda and so I did some checking, and unfortunately I have verified that what I heard is the truth." Leaning forward, Sylvia said, "You need to know that Brenda has been working elsewhere on our company time. She has been doing modeling on weekends at a fashion house, which of course is none of our business. But when you were away, she picked up some extra hours there. On the day of your departmental presentation, she called in to say her mother had an emergency."

"How do you know that she didn't?" Ellen asked.

"Because Marion ... you know, our fashion reporter ... was at the show that day. She saw Brenda walking the runway."

Ellen sank back in her chair. "This explains a lot. Her tardiness, her mistakes."

Nodding her head, Sylvia continued, "And can you believe she made that hundred-thousand-dollar error?"

"Hundred-thousand-dollar error?" Ellen was hoping that she had misheard Sylvia.

"I guess Nick hasn't had a chance to tell you. Brenda made some major typos, including adding a few zeros where they didn't belong, turning your budget request into an astronomical, off-the-chart amount."

"A hundred thousand?" Ellen echoed. The figure was so absurd Marc would have known it was an error at once. Ellen remembered Nick wanted to tell her something the night before but she had cut him off.

"And Nick corrected the mistakes," Ellen said, thinking how easy it would have been for Nick to have let it go, making her look ridiculous. But he hadn't.

Ellen shook her head. "To think I bought Brenda's story about her sick mother."

"How would you have known otherwise, Ellen? You have no right to pry into an employee's family life."

Ellen looked at Sylvia. "What do I do next?"

Sylvia smiled grimly. "You get to fire Brenda."

CHAPTER THIRTY-ONE

Directly from work, Ellen walked four blocks to the Italian restaurant, stopping only to make a few purchases at a five-and-ten-cent store. She bought a hair comb, a gold-toned eye shadow, and inexpensive glass earrings.

In the ladies' room at the restaurant, she took off her jacket, washed her face, and applied the eye shadow. Awkwardly, she twisted her hair into a bun, managed to fix the comb into it, and then put on the earrings, hoping the glue holding the baubles would last at least for a few hours.

She thought the bun gave her a harsh look, so she pulled down a few strands of hair over each ear and was pleased to see they curled into tendrils naturally. *Some benefits to being way overdue for a haircut,* she thought, applying dark pink lipstick which she always carried in her bag but seldom used. Her cheeks were still flushed from the walk, giving her face some natural color.

Ellen loosened the collar of her blouse and undid the top two buttons. The blouse was fitted, making it easy to pull out so it fell just below her waistline. The adjustment allowed her to hike up her skirt another inch, and she hoped her sensible walking shoes might not look as frumpy. *This little maneuver gives my legs more shape*, she thought, smiling as she posed sideways before the full-length mirror.

She felt herself lightening up after the worst work day in her life. There had been no choice but to let Brenda go, Ellen's first time terminating an employee. She thought Brenda was expecting it, which made it easier, but still, it had felt awful and Ellen fervently hoped she'd never have to fire anyone else.

Leaving the ladies' room, her jacket draped over her arm which covered up the bulky shoulder bag, she heard a low whistle, and felt a familiar touch on her arm.

"Is this gorgeous creature the same harried lady I saw this afternoon?" Nick whispered, leaning down and brushing a light kiss on the side of her neck.

Turning so quickly that her lips almost touched his, she said, "I don't remember seeing you at all this afternoon."

Nick straightened and took both her hands. "That's because when I saw you stepping out of the elevator, I didn't dash down the hall to touch your elbow, which used to get me into trouble," he said with a smile. Then he quickly turned serious. "Look, I'm sorry if I made you uncomfortable. You've had enough problems in the workplace without my adding to it."

"You heard about Brenda?"

"Oh, yeah, I saw her emptying her desk."

After the maître'd led them to the table and they were seated, Nick said, "You look so fantastic, those guys at the bar are staring at you."

Picking up her menu, Ellen smiled. "And can you imagine the nerve of that guy who just whistled at me when I came out of the ladies' room?"

"I would say that guy has very good taste."

Ellen put aside her menu. "We need to have a serious talk, Nick. Now is as good as ever."

"I already told you I understand. I promise not to act like a school boy with a crush on the teacher."

"Are you sure that's not what this is?" she asked, half-afraid to hear the answer.

He grinned. "I'm not attracted to you because I work for you, Ellen, if that's what you mean. That would really take the fun out of my pursuing you."

"Nick, the point is that regardless of our positions at work, or who works for whom, we both ... well, we want the same thing." She faltered, knowing her face was flushed, then continued. "But I can't imagine how we can spend the night together and then conduct business as usual the next morning."

"I totally agree."

"You do?"

Grinning, he said, "Just Friday and Saturday nights then. And holidays."

"I'm serious. We won't get anywhere if we make light of it."

"Okay, we have a problem, and I have a solution."

"What's that?"

"Fire me."

Despite herself, Ellen laughed. "On what grounds?"

"Sickness. Love sickness."

"You can't be fired for an illness, Nick Stanton. You know that."

He sighed. "And now I can't even mess up at work so you can terminate me, because Brenda's beat me to it. Besides, I wouldn't do that to you."

"Why not?" she asked, still smiling, picking up her water glass.

"First of all, firing two employees in a week wouldn't look good on your personnel record. But most important, I, Nicholas Everett Stanton, am falling more in love with you every day, Ellen Von Der Hyde." Looking at his watch, he added, "Actually, by the minute. I am now one hour more in love with you since we were seated at this table."

The ice chips in Ellen's glass made a clinking sound. Her smile faded. Nick placed his hand over her shaking hand.

"I didn't plan to say that tonight. I got carried away. First things, first, though. Here comes our dinner."

The waiter placed steaming plates of pasta and shrimp in front of each of them. "This is the most popular entree on our menu," the waiter said, with a slight bow. "May I tell you the story behind it?"

"Please do," said Ellen, relieved for the chance to change the subject.

"The chef who created this dish is a pure romantic at heart. He said that when both the lady and the gentleman order this at the very same time, it means they are either a married couple or will be within a very short time."

"My compliments to the chef," said Nick, raising his glass. "I couldn't be more pleased."

Neither could I, thought Ellen. *But I'm not about to admit it.*

❧

In front of her building, Nick leaned down to kiss Ellen but suddenly whispered, "Watch it, there's someone coming up behind you." He pulled Ellen behind him, shielding her as a woman in a long coat came out of the shadows. "Don't you come any closer," Nick warned.

Ellen saw just enough of the woman's face to recognize her. "Theresa!" she cried out. "How in the world did you get here?"

Theresa held out her hand, palm up. In it was Ellen's business card. "You gave me your address," she said.

"Yes, I know. But how did you get here?"

"My mother loved city life. Sometimes she took me and my sister to the theaters, and the circus when it came to town. I took the train, just like we used to do. It's been a very long time."

Nick, releasing Ellen's arm, said with relief, "See? All roads lead to the circus."

Ellen sighed. "Nick, this is Theresa, and Theresa, this is my friend Nick."

Smiling, Nick said, "I'm glad to finally meet you, Theresa." Turning to Ellen, he said, "'Did you say 'my friend Nick'? I'm not your boyfriend?"

Theresa let out a cry. "You called me Theresa. How do you know my name?"

In a firm voice, Ellen said, "I'll tell you how I found out your name when we go inside. But first you have to assure me that you'll tell the truth."

"I don't have any reason to lie," Theresa said. "Because my words can't hurt anyone anymore. Everyone is gone, you see."

With a sigh, Ellen turned to Nick. "I'm so sorry to end the evening on this note, but I have so many questions that only Theresa can answer."

Putting his arms around Ellen, Nick said, "Of course. This might be your only chance. This lady is an elusive soul." He eyed Theresa warily. "I guess she's harmless. But still, take good care of yourself, okay?"

"I will," Ellen said. But she had no fear of Theresa. All she had was curiosity—and the hope that she would finally get some answers.

&♣.

A flash of lightning streaked across the long windows, followed by a crashing rain. Theresa set her burlap bag under the table by the door and saw the three silver-framed photos. "Oh, that's Eric," she said, "and your parents." Picking up the third picture, she said, "Who are these people?"

"That's my sister, Meg, and her husband and children," Ellen explained.

"Eric used to mention you, but not another sister."

"That's because Meg wasn't born yet. There are eight years

between us." Ellen took the photograph from Theresa's hands. "Come, let's sit down."

Theresa sat across from Ellen at the dinette table, her hands folded together, as if preparing to be interrogated. Ellen thought back to the way Theresa had looked at the cemetery. Her eyes had shown fear, pain, and sadness. Now, she thought, there was still pain and sadness, but the fear was gone.

Ellen said, "It's so late, and with this rainstorm, I hope you'll stay overnight. I'll take out the folding cot that's in the closet and make it up for you. Any other items you might need are in the bathroom closet."

"Thank you," Theresa whispered. Then she astounded Ellen by saying, "I came to tell you that Chief Lake died, of a heart attack. You won't be called in for more questioning."

"What? How would you know anything about the chief's death?"

"Because I went to his house three days ago, and I knew right away he'd been drinking, but we talked a little anyway. Then he got angry with me, so I left. The next day, I went to the police station to talk, thinking he'd be recovered by then. But when I asked at the desk for him, a policeman took me to a room, and there were detectives there, and they were very kind, and told me that he died of a heart attack. I learned that you had been questioned, but no one knew that he had heart problems and was scheduled for more cardiac tests until after he died."

"Wait a minute." Ellen's eyes narrowed as she studied Theresa, wondering if she had greatly underestimated her. "You knew the chief of police well enough that you actually went to his house?"

"Yes," Theresa said quietly.

Ellen began to put the pieces together, remembering a photo that Meg had found in the yearbook. "Did you have a sister by the name of Victoria Lake?"

"Yes," said Theresa.

"You said your mother liked big cities. Was she married to Police Chief Lake?"

Theresa nodded.

"Then the chief, he was your father?"

Looking away, Theresa again nodded.

"But why is your sister's class photo in the yearbook and not yours?"

"Because my father sent me away to boarding school," Theresa explained. "He didn't want me to be anything like Victoria. He thought he was doing the right thing."

"Why do you go by the name of Theresa Francis?"

"It was Theresa Francis Lake," she mumbled, "until my father disowned me when he found out I was pregnant. He couldn't handle more shame, so he took me out of boarding school and arranged for me to work full time in the monastery kitchen. I hardly saw the monks because I lived in a separate building. It was ideal for my father, because the monks would never say a word, about anything, of course. And Rose, she's the cook there, was very closemouthed and protective of me."

Ellen decided not to mention yet that she had met with Rose. "So hardly anyone from Springton would remember you."

"The boarding school was just far enough away, in a big town. And I was very quiet, not like Victoria. No one in Springton would have missed me."

"Where was the boarding school?" Ellen asked, already guessing the answer.

"Keaton," Theresa said.

Ellen stood and paced, like a lawyer in a courtroom. "Of course, Keaton." she muttered.

Theresa nodded. "It was an overpopulated town, filled with people from all over, who come and go, a town that has schools, and colleges, and hospitals."

And the Community Church, Ellen almost blurted out. "It was perfect. You would be a little fish in a big pond. And even if someone caught on to your last name, it wouldn't have meant anything to them. Your father was the police chief of Springton, not Keaton."

Theresa gave a small smile. "Of course."

A thought crossed Ellen's mind. She stood still and gazed out at the driving rain washing down the streets. She allowed her thoughts to drift back to the man who towered like a giant in her bedroom doorway so many years ago.

Police Chief Lake.

Turning to Theresa, she said, "I saw a portrait of your father at the police station. He was heavyset. Was he thin when he was younger?"

Theresa nodded. "I was surprised at how much weight he had gained."

From a stranger whose face Ellen hadn't recognized when she was a little girl, Chief Lake was now a man of many faces. A man whose daughter had been carrying Ellen's brother's baby, a man who'd abused his power to the extent her parents felt threatened enough to send their son away and sign away their estate.

A controlling man who would have known where his daughter's baby was buried.

Ellen had thought she would be satisfied just to learn the identity of this woman sitting in her kitchen, but now she realized, to her dismay, it was only the beginning.

Theresa was saying, "All I want is a marker for my baby's grave."

Ellen sat down and took Theresa's hand. "You've got to tell me what makes you think the baby is buried in my family's plot. I need to know that."

Twisting her hands, Theresa said, "When I gave birth, I was coming out of the anesthesia and the doctor said I had a baby girl and she was a stillborn. I didn't understand what that meant, and he explained that she had died. I became hysterical and he put a needle in my arm. Before I went back to sleep, I saw two women next to my bed. One of them whispered, "Esther and Rudolph Von Der Hyde are ready to tend to things now."

Ellen tried to picture the scene. "And by that, you thought they meant the baby's burial would be in the Von Der Hyde plot?"

"Of course. What else could it be?"

"I don't know," Ellen admitted.

"You have to understand," Theresa said. "Although my father wasn't observant of his faith, his family plot was in a strict religious cemetery in Leighton." Ellen knew Leighton was a small town just outside of Springton. "That cemetery wouldn't have allowed a baby born out of wedlock. The Von Der Hydes would have made sure the baby was buried in their family plot."

"Back to the two women at your bedside, do you know who they were?" Ellen asked gently.

"I remember they were wearing black dresses. I don't think I saw their faces."

Ellen tucked this information away in her mind, and said, "Is there anything else that made you think the baby was buried in my family's plot?"

"Oh, yes. When Eric came home four years ago for your parents' funeral, he visited the Pomarium on some business. Then he came around to the kitchen to see Rose. He was shocked to see me there. He thought I'd gone off to nursing school. Which is what I wanted to do before ... the pregnancy."

"What happened when you saw him?"

"We stared at each other, like two strangers. Eric suggested we take a walk in the orchard, so that's what we did. And then, right near the tree where we used to meet, I blurted out everything. How I had the baby, that she was a stillborn, and since he would likely be handling his parents' grave markers, it was only right he get one for the baby. Our baby Rose.

"Eric was stunned, and his face turned pale. He asked me to believe that he never knew I was pregnant, that he would have found a way for us to marry if only he had known.

"He began to pace, like you just did, Ellen. I think he said something about his parents leaving money to the monastery, that's why he was there. I don't know anything about that. He asked me the date of our baby's birth, and I told him March 17, 1930. I was sure he asked so the date on the marker would be correct.

"And then he stopped pacing, and it was like a shock went through him. He reached out for the tree, to steady himself. He said that his military commitment would end in five years, and he would come back here and handle everything at that time. He said that anything he did now would affect many lives, and infuriate my father, making it harder for me. And there would be nothing he could do because he would be gone again. Eric said he wouldn't let that happen twice."

"What do you think he meant?" Ellen asked.

"My father had a terrible temper," Theresa explained. "He would fly into rages. I always wondered if he had something else against your family ... aside from the fact that I was having Eric's baby. But he once said he would have burned your house down if he thought he could get away with it."

Ellen's thoughts came as rapidly as the pellets of rain striking the window. *Instead of burning the house, he found another way of getting it,* Ellen realized, *by biding his time and making sure the estate was left to the monastery. Whether my mother and father really knew that Theresa was housed in the monastery, and their money was payback, is a secret taken to their graves. They would have done exactly as the chief wanted to protect their family.*

"But you still haven't answered my question. Why do you think the baby is in the Von Der Hyde plot?"

"Before Eric left, he held my hands and said, 'I just figured something out, Theresa, and want you to try to find comfort in what I'm about to tell you. My parents were compassionate and responsible people. They would have done the right thing for our baby. That's all I can tell you right now. I'm sorry.'"

"And by that, you assumed they gave your baby a burial in the Von Der Hyde plot?" *How trusting and innocent this girl is,* Ellen thought, *to think her father would have given permission for her parents, the very people he hated, to take the baby for burial.*

"Of course. What else could he have meant?"

Ellen thought back to her visit with Harvey. She remembered thinking he knew more than he let on. Her words came out fast. "Have you gone back to your father's house?"

Theresa shook her head. "No. I don't want to go there."

"But someone needs to find his paperwork. Things like his will, insurance, and property deeds are very important."

An idea seemed to come to Theresa. "Maybe my baby is buried in another cemetery, and the papers are in my father's house." She took a tarnished brass key ring out of her pocketbook. "I don't know why I kept my house keys, maybe as a reminder that I had a home once."

"So you'll go back to the house?" Ellen asked, trying not to let her excitement show.

"Yes, but I don't want to go in there alone. Eric was supposed to take care of everything, and that's impossible now." Theresa's eyes were glassy with tears. "You're his sister, the closest person I have now. Will you go with me?"

Ellen nodded. "I'll go with you tomorrow, but first, there's someone you should call. I learned your name from Rose Flanagan. She's worried about you. I want you to call her first thing in the morning."

Theresa nodded. "Yes, I will call Rose. She's been my family all these years."

CHAPTER THIRTY-TWO

Wednesday, March 16

There were no household noises in the morning, making Ellen think Theresa had disappeared again.

Instead, Theresa was sitting at the dinette table, as still as she was at the cemetery. She clutched the phone. Gone was the light in her eyes of the night before. She stared straight ahead, not seeming to be aware of Ellen standing in front of her.

Ellen gently took the phone and placed it in the receiver. "Theresa, what's wrong?"

"Rose is dead," Theresa answered in a flat voice.

"That can't be," Ellen said. "She was the picture of health when I saw her. Whoever told you that?"

"I called Rose's number a little while ago and was transferred to the director. She told me that Rose didn't come to work and so they checked on her and found her dead in her chair. It's my fault. I should have been there."

"Don't do this to yourself," Ellen said. "It's not your fault."

"I don't know how she died. The director said toxicology tests are being done."

"Did she say why?"

"She said there was some foam around Rose's lips. That's all she knew. She also said I am welcome to go back there."

Ellen held Theresa's hands, which were ice cold. "Theresa, you've had way too many losses in your life, and now there are three more, in a very short time. That's too much for anyone to bear on their own. Maybe there's someone who works at the home who will help you.

"We'll take the train first thing tomorrow and go directly to the home. You can be with people you know and talk to someone. Will you please do that?"

"No. I need to get to my father's house first."

"But it might be too much. I'm worried about you."

"It needs to be done," Theresa said with no emotion. "If there are no answers for me in that house, where my life began, then I will go back to the Pomarium and work there until my life ends. Just like Rose."

CHAPTER THIRTY-THREE

Wednesday, March 16

Springton, Massachusetts

The kitchen door of Lake's house squeaked when Theresa turned the key in the rusty lock. The kitchen smelled like grease. There were dirty dishes and pans on the countertop.

"My sister, Meg, would have a fit if she saw this," said Ellen.

"Does Meg live in Boston too?"

"Heavens, no. Meg married her high school sweetheart, Carl Anderson, and they live right here in Springton, in the same house Carl grew up in."

Theresa's eyes brightened. "I know that house. I babysat there a few times."

"That's where I stay when I'm in town," said Ellen. "It's a small world."

"It's good to have a sister." Theresa's voice became flatter, quieter. "I had a sister once, but no more. I had a mother once, but no more. I had a father— "

"Please, don't do this to yourself," Ellen broke in. "Why don't you keep searching, and I'll do these dishes?" She gave Theresa an encouraging smile and nodded to a door off the kitchen. "There might be some old boxes of files in the cellar."

Theresa put on the light switch and went down the stairs. Moments later, a high-pitched scream sent Ellen hurrying into the basement. Theresa was staring at an antique jelly cupboard. The lock had been torn off and the surrounding wood trim smashed in. The hand-carved door dangled by one hinge, exposing rows of fruit jelly jars on glass shelves.

"This belonged to my grandmother Lake," Theresa cried. "She said it would be mine someday. It's wrecked now."

"Nothing else in the house looks as if it was vandalized," Ellen said, puzzled. "Maybe there's something they wanted in there?"

Theresa reached in and took a jar of dark-colored jelly from the top shelf and held it up to the light filtering through the dusty cellar window. "This is over twenty years old," she said. "It shouldn't be left around. People could get sick."

She threw it against the concrete wall. The heavy jar shattered when it hit, and the smell of rotted fruit wafted across the room. One at a time, Theresa hurled jars of jelly, saying in a chant-like tone, that each one was for the losses in her life.

Ellen put out her hand to stop her and then thought better of it. *Maybe it's time for you to show some anger, Theresa,* she thought. *Maybe by getting it all out, you'll get back into the world.*

Finally spent, Theresa knelt before the cupboard and removed a jar from the bottom shelf. Holding it close to her, she opened it and inhaled, then held it up to Ellen, who could smell the sweet fragrance of peaches from where she stood.

Cradling the jar, Theresa said that her baby was conceived during the peach season. She was smiling, showing her star-shaped dimples. Ellen moved closer to the jelly cupboard and noticed an envelope, tied with a string, behind the gap left by the jar of peach preserves. She reached for it and handed it to Theresa. "You go upstairs, sit down, and read what's in here, and I'll clean up this mess."

Minutes later, Theresa called down to Ellen. "It's all in here!" she shouted, waving the papers in her hand.

"What is? Your father's will?"

"No! The truth is in here! They lied to me! My baby is alive! She was adopted!"

"Theresa, stay right there!" Ellen called back, but the sticky mass of jelly slowed her as she made her way up the stairs. "Don't you leave, Theresa, do you hear me? Don't go!"

Cleaning the bottom of her shoes and carefully gripping the stair rail, Ellen made it to the first floor, too late. The kitchen door was wide open. The envelope was on the table, ripped open and empty. There was no sign of Theresa.

This time she's not running away, Ellen thought. *This time Theresa is running to someone. And that someone is connected to the contents of that envelope.*

Ellen dialed Meg's number from Chief Lake's wall phone and asked her to pick her up. Ellen had forgotten that Meg didn't know she was back in Springton.

"You're at the police chief's house?" Meg asked, her voice nearly cracking with disbelief. "What did you do, break in?"

"Of course not," Ellen said quickly. "But now we know the name of the woman who visits Eric's grave. Her name is Theresa and she's Chief Lake's daughter. We went to the house to find papers. She had the key and let me in. I have so much to tell you."

"I'm leaving now," Meg said, hanging up.

Relieved that Meg didn't give her a lecture, Ellen went out the back door, locking it behind her. She wished she could put everything else behind her, but it was too late.

Ellen's relief at no lecture was short-lived. "I really don't understand why you didn't let me know you were coming back to Springton," Meg said, moments after Ellen got into the car.

"Besides, you look a mess." Meg gave a sniff. "And why do you smell like peaches? It's not the season."

"Not now, Meg," said Ellen, slumping back in the seat.

Meg wasn't finished. "And I know all about you going to Julian's office. He said you were very pushy, and that the only reason he tolerated it was because of his friendship with Eric."

"And not because of his friendship with you?"

Meg looked exasperated. "I don't know what you mean. Julian's like family to me. Carl has relatives here, and I have no one."

"I'd like *not* to think I'm no one, Meg," Ellen said quietly.

"You know what I mean. No family nearby. But to get back to my point, that strange woman left you stranded in a house where our police chief was found dead. In the eyes of the law, you may have been trespassing." Meg nervously tapped her fingers on the steering wheel. "I hope no one saw you."

"Well, if someone did, you will certainly hear about it," Ellen replied, with a note of sarcasm. Why was her sister acting like this? She seemed to think that Ellen was going to disgrace her. Which, Ellen realized, was exactly what the chief had thought about his daughter. Ellen was getting extremely tired of all these people being so obsessed with their own reputations.

Ellen glanced at her watch. She had missed the last train back to Boston. Which meant spending the night at Meg's. She just hoped that Meg wouldn't invite Julian over.

CHAPTER THIRTY-FOUR

With the adoption papers in her hand, Theresa ran until she could run no more. Leaning against a telephone pole and catching her breath, she turned and walked slowly back to her father's house. As much as she liked Ellen, she was hoping she was gone. She unlocked the door, and to her relief, the house was empty. The jelly was all cleaned up, and she felt bad but not as bad as she felt when she read the adoption papers. A lie on top of another lie. She knew something her father didn't know.

The adoption papers were phony.

Only twenty-four hours earlier, Theresa would have believed every word in the paperwork. But that was before she learned Ellen had a sister in Springton, and before she saw the photo of Meg's family in Ellen's apartment.

Theresa went through a few closets until she found a box of black-and-white photos. Sitting in the straight-backed chair her father used to sit in, she found the exact one she was looking for, herself at age four. Then she dug through her burlap bag and took out the photo of Meg's family that she had slipped out of the silver frame in Ellen's apartment. It was the first thing she had ever taken from anyone in her life, but she had convinced herself she was just borrowing it.

She set her childhood photo next to the little girl in the picture. There it was: both photos showed identical star-shaped dimples. *She's a little me*, thought Theresa, realizing now that Eric had discovered the secret four years ago when she told him she had given birth to their daughter. He didn't tell her the baby had lived. And she understood why. He couldn't stay to help pick up the pieces.

She knew what she had to do.

CHAPTER THIRTY-FIVE

In the hallway, Meg and Ellen took their shoes off. It was mud season in Springton. Meg pulled out slippers that she kept in the front closet, and said, "I'm not sure I want to do this anymore."

Ellen said, "You really don't want to know why Mom and Dad left everything to a church in Keaton? You're the one who brought up the subject of the inheritance, not me."

Meg handed Ellen a pair of pink fluffy slippers. "Oh, Ellen, you have no idea how many times I've wished I could take back those words. Like Julian says, sometimes it's best if we let the dead take their secrets to the grave."

"What would be best is that we don't discuss Julian anymore," Ellen snapped.

At Meg's look of annoyance, Ellen said, "All right. Yes, I should have called to tell you I was back in town. My plans were to go back to Boston tonight. But here I am, without so much as a toothbrush." She put on the slippers. They were way too big. She shuffled down the hall to the kitchen. "I'm going to call in a story to my paper. Will you let me borrow some overnight things?"

"Of course." Meg nodded and went upstairs.

Ellen called Nick at the office. Answering on the first ring, he asked about what was going on in Springton. "I'll fill you in later," she said, then quickly turned to business. She was glad to turn her mind to things that mattered to her in Boston, to hear Nick say things were going well and that Nigel had taken photos to go with her story on homeless women.

"I think it's what you're looking for," he said. "Nigel saw a woman panhandling during the noon hour. When she had enough coins, she went into a restaurant and came out with a sandwich. Then she went to a doorway and shared it with another lady.

"Nigel got talking to her, and she let him take the photos," Nick went on. "She was eager to tell her story. She told him that her children planned to put her away about a year ago, but she'd rather die than lose her freedom. She's been on the streets ever since. Nigel said there was something dignified about her, in spite of her situation. That's what came out in the pictures, Ellen. You were right in pushing Nigel."

It was the second time in an hour that she had been told in one way or another that she was pushy. *Maybe women aren't supposed to be pushy,* she thought, *but it's useful when you want to learn things.*

"How did things go with Theresa?" asked Nick.

"Good in one way, because she found some important papers. But bad in another, because she's run away again."

"I was afraid of that happening."

"Look, I missed the last train to Boston, so I'm going to stay another night," said Ellen. "I'll be back sometime tomorrow and tell you more when we get together."

"Over dinner," Nick said, lowering his voice. "At the Italian restaurant. You know, the one where the chef can read our future. We'll order the same entree."

Leave it to Nick to make me forget this whole mess, even for a few minutes, she thought.

Grinning, she said, "Actually, I've been craving a Boston hot dog, from one of the street-corner wagons."

"On one condition," he said.

"What would that be?"

"No onions."

Later, Ellen rinsed her blouse and hung it up to dry in the bathroom. After her shower, she put on a pair of flannel pajamas and chenille robe that belonged to Meg. Beth and Matthew came into her bedroom with books, and she read stories until their eyes began to close. After she tucked them into their own beds, she went back into her room and drifted off to a peaceful sleep, dreaming about peach orchards.

CHAPTER THIRTY-SIX

Ellen's blouse wasn't hanging in the bathroom the next morning. She followed the aroma of coffee downstairs and found Meg ironing it in the kitchen.

"There," Meg said, pressing the iron down hard on a sleeve. "That crease will stay in for a while." She held the blouse out to Ellen. "This is my thanks for getting Beth and Matthew to sleep last night," she said, smiling. "I don't want you to rush off, Ellen. Will you stay today?"

"I'd like to. I can work from here. But, first I'm going to the cemetery to see if there are any roses on the grave. That may tell me if Theresa's still around."

Meg turned to pull a shirt out of the laundry basket. "You're welcome to take my car. The car keys are on the hall table." With a wry smile, she added, "You may remember which table ... the one with the vase that used to have dried flowers in it."

Ellen winced. "I was worried about you finding the flowers all crushed," she confessed. "I'm sorry. I'll find a florist and replace them."

"Don't bother," Meg said, waving her hand. "It's a relief that I don't need to keep that hideous vase out anymore. It was headed for the spring yard sale at the school, believe me."

Ellen and Meg burst out laughing at the same time.

Ellen felt something inside her relax. Maybe Meg wasn't ready to hear about their parents' wills or Theresa's connection to Eric, Ellen thought. But she and Meg were growing closer, and for the first time she was sure that together, they would weather whatever secrets she might uncover.

Instead of going through the main road that would take her directly to the cemetery, Ellen backtracked and drove to her old house, the one where she grew up. Nothing had changed on the twisting backroads that led there. It was as if time had stood still. She thought about the bustling city of Boston, the new walkways linking museums and theaters and restaurants. She missed all of it. Her own life was on hold. If she didn't find Theresa today, she would commute on weekends, follow her own leads, and not push Meg anymore.

The cluster of lilac trees ahead meant that her old house was just around the bend. Ellen hadn't seen it since it was sold after her parents' death.

When she saw the two-story home, her first thought was that she had taken a wrong turn. Slowing down, she saw the original bungalow was still there, with additions to the left and right sides that replaced more than half of her father's beloved lilac trees. The upstairs bedrooms had finally been finished; she could see dormer windows with gingham curtains in them. A child's tricycle was in the driveway that was now paved.

Life continues on Lilac Lane, she thought. *I wonder what lies ahead for this family*. Remembering the many times she had ridden her own bicycle up the gravel driveway, stubbornly gripping the handlebars, all in defiance of her mother who told her to walk it up so she wouldn't fall and scrape her knees, Ellen blinked back the tears. Her mother was now forever at the destination Ellen was now driving to—the cemetery.

At the gravesite, the ground was muddy, and there was no evidence of a rose, not even a remnant of the petals that Theresa had last placed. A gnawing feeling tugged at Ellen as she walked around the tombstone.

What had Theresa found in the envelope? Whom could she go to? Was it any of Ellen's business?

She cupped her hands around her mouth. "Theresa!" she yelled, hearing her voice resonating across the hollow. But no one answered. And Ellen had an awful feeling that Theresa was gone —and with her the answers to the mysteries that began with her brother Eric and Chief Lake.

CHAPTER THIRTY-SEVEN

When Ellen returned to her sister's house, she wasn't surprised to find Meg bustling in the kitchen. Ellen watched her add a cup of cocoa into a bowl with flour and sugar. "Oh," Ellen said, "you're making a cake. And it's not out of a box?"

"Not in this kitchen." Meg laughed. "It's a birthday cake. While you were gone, I got to thinking that Beth's birthday party with her little friends isn't until next week. But since you're here now, I thought it would be nice to have a family dinner tonight, with a little party for Beth afterward. I've invited Carl's Aunt Ruth and his Uncle Stan, and of course, Julian, and ... oh, stop it," she said, noticing the face Ellen made when she heard Julian's name. Meg continued, "Best of all, we have a mystery guest."

Impulsively, Ellen asked, "Is it Theresa?"

Meg gave her an irritated look. "Will you please give it up? Of course not. I invited Nick Stanton. He said he'd leave for Springton right after work. Isn't that wonderful? And he'll drive you back to Boston tonight."

Meg turned to add butter to the mixing bowl, and Ellen was glad that she didn't see her wide smile and the warm blush creeping into her cheeks. Ellen couldn't believe it. Nick was driving here for a four-year old's birthday party?

Meg's enthusiasm was contagious. Ellen wanted to pitch in and help with the dinner and didn't mind at all when Meg gave her simple things to do. Meg let her set the table and then blow up balloons and hang them with streamers from the ceiling. Ellen got into the spirit of the birthday party enough to put aside her worry about Theresa, at least for a while.

Later, after Meg had refolded the napkins and rearranged the plates Ellen had set out, Meg deftly frosted the cake with chocolate icing and arranged miniature figures of tigers, lions, and elephants on top. "It's a zoo theme," she explained, handing Ellen the bowl of leftover frosting. She smiled as Ellen ran a spoon around the rim and then licked the chocolate off. "Beth will be so pleased to see Nick," said Meg. "She still talks about him, and his stories about the city. Why, I wouldn't be surprised if he brings her an elephant from the zoo to go with all those peanuts."

The thought of Nick coming in the front door with a present for her niece created a warm stirring within Ellen. She thought of how he had rushed to her apartment when she had the dream and remembered the strength of his warm arms. Once again, he was going out of his way to see her.

She watched her sister move confidently around the kitchen, first basting the roast, next tossing a huge salad, then going through the cupboards to find just the right hiding place for the cake. She was a carbon copy of their mother, except for the fact that Meg had a more cheerful nature, while Esther Von Der Hyde was mostly worried and serious.

Which am I? wondered Ellen. *I was happy when I moved to Boston,* she realized. *Now I'm worried and serious, like our mother. I want to be happy again.*

"Meg," she said, "let's have fun and play some games tonight, like pin the tail on the donkey. I think Beth and Matthew would like that."

"That would be great." Then, with a mischievous smile, Meg added, "But the front doorbell just rang. Will you get it?"

Ellen wanted to run down the hallway, but with the floppy slippers on her feet, she didn't need Nick to see her fall flat on her face. When she opened the door and saw him standing there, with a smile on his face, and holding a stuffed elephant that was half as tall as he was, a tear ran down her cheek.

He let the elephant drop, stepped through the doorway, and drew her to him. "Hey, what's the matter?" he murmured into her ear. Lifting her chin, he kissed her lightly, then more strongly when she returned it. A low groan came from deep within his throat before he pulled away.

"I want some time with you alone," he said, then drew her closer again and kissed her all over her cheeks.

"Tonight," Ellen whispered in between kisses. "My apartment. We'll leave right after the party."

At the sound of Meg's footsteps, Ellen pulled herself away but was unable to talk. She was sure all her breath had been transferred to Nick.

"Why, Meg," Nick said, as if he was surprised that she would be in her own house. His voice was husky. Clearing his throat, he said, "Thanks for inviting me."

"I hope I haven't interrupted anything," Meg said, grinning. She pointed to the open door. "I think you left someone very important out on the porch."

Straightening his shirt collar, Nick drew a blank, then laughed. "Oh, my gosh, I forgot Ellie."

"Ellie?" Ellen repeated. "You named a stuffed elephant for me?"

"Sort of," he said sheepishly. "You were my inspiration."

Ellen smoothed down her hair while Nick opened the door and picked up the elephant. "Don't worry," he said, "she won't eat much."

Giving Ellen a knowing "I told you so" look, and obviously enjoying herself, Meg said, "I'll hide Ellie in the pantry."

"Do I ever love chocolate frosting," said Nick while Ellen hung up his jacket.

"How do you know we're having chocolate?" Ellen asked.

"By your sweet lips. Why did you think I wanted to keep kissing you? Besides," he said, looking at her floppy slippers, "I never kissed the Easter bunny before."

❦

The sounds of utensils striking against the sides of serving bowls punctuated the noises of chatter and laughter made by the seven adults and two children gathered around the huge oak table.

Oh, I so appreciate my beautiful family, Ellen thought. She lifted slices of pot roast smothered in gravy and onions from a platter to her plate. She had managed to put away all her concerns and was thoroughly enjoying the birthday dinner.

Beth and Mathew had insisted on sitting on either side of Nick, leaving Ellen to sit directly across the table from him, with Julian to the right side of her and Carl's sister, Ruth, on the other. She was pleased to sit across from Nick, so she could watch his ease with the children. He had completely fit in with Carl's family, especially with Ruth's husband, Stan, who had lived in Boston for a short time. Nick and Stan entertained the others with humorous stories about city life.

Julian was reserved, speaking just enough to be polite. When Ellen had enough of his curt answers in response to her few casual questions, she turned to Carl's sister.

"Ruth, you might like to know that Julian drove me out to visit Harvey Poston the other day. It's the first time we've met. He's certainly an interesting man."

Frowning, Ruth said, "Come to think of it, we haven't seen Harvey in town lately. Tell me, how is he doing?"

"He seems to be having a hard time with some things, like finances—"

"Harvey's just fine," Julian interrupted, reaching across Ellen for a biscuit. Ripping the biscuit in half, he said, "Ellen, will you please pass the butter?" When she handed it to him, he leaned in close and whispered, "I hardly think talking about Harvey's money problems is conversation for a child's birthday party."

"Oh, really? What about his medical issues?" she whispered back, then bit her lip. Meg had worked hard for this dinner and she was not going to let Julian provoke her.

Ruth smiled at Julian. "It was very thoughtful of you to drive Ellen out to visit Harvey. The poor man was so lost when his wife, Margaret, died. He's such a lonely figure when he comes into town with his dog. But you're sure Harvey is all right?"

Julian, buttering his roll, nodded. "He's just as eccentric as ever."

"I don't think Harvey Poston was ever eccentric," said Stan, smiling. "Margaret wouldn't have allowed it."

"I completely agree," said Carl.

Ruth frowned again. "Seriously, one of us should stop in some day. Margaret would certainly expect that of us. After all, she was there for everyone else. A true community person. If it weren't for her, it would have taken ages for this town to have a Red Cross chapter." Beaming at Julian, Ruth said, "Let's follow Julian's fine example, and check in with our elderly. I'm going to get some people together and start a visitation list. We have you to thank for starting this process, Julian. That was very nice of you to go out of your way."

Turning slightly to smile at Ellen, Julian graciously accepted the compliment. "It was my pleasure, Ruth."

Ellen looked away.

Beth blew out the candles on her cake. She opened several gaily wrapped boxes of assorted clothes and toys, then gave out a delighted shriek when she spotted the stuffed elephant, which was supposedly out of sight in the pantry, but had tilted enough to be visible. Beth jumped out of her chair and ran to the elephant, then dragged it back to the table where she placed it between herself and Nick.

"Oh, I love you," said Beth.

"Why, thank you," said Nick.

"No, I mean him," she said, pointing to the elephant.

"It's a her, silly," he said. "For you to name. Now, you open the rest of your presents, and I'll take good care of your elephant."

Ellen put Julian out of her mind. She was happy to be in the midst of her family, and even happier that Nick was there, fitting in as if he'd been part of them all his life. In one way, she didn't want the evening to end, but in another she couldn't stand the wait until she would finally be in his arms. Nick gave her a grin that reflected her own thoughts. *We'll be together finally. Tonight.*

Beth began rubbing her eyes, and leaned against the elephant, which was propped against Nick.

"Just one more present to open," said Meg, holding up the last package, a long white box wrapped with pink satin ribbon. "It's from Julian."

"Saving the best for last," said Julian. Beth reluctantly let go of the elephant and, with her mother's help, opened the box. Ellen glanced sideways at Julian, who was watching intently. When she followed his fixed look, she realized it wasn't the little girl he was watching.

Julian was staring hard at Meg, who was radiant and flushed. Just above Nick's head, an antique mirror hung over the sideboard, allowing Ellen to see Julian's expression turn from one of interest to one of something else.

What was she seeing on Julian's face? she wondered. Admiration? No. Something much more intense. She couldn't believe the thoughts that were racing through her mind. *What's the matter with me?* she wondered.

Then she saw it. And knew for certain. There was no doubt in

Ellen's mind. Julian was gazing at her sister, all right. With love. In Meg's very own home, at her own table, with her husband, and children. Meg, totally happy. Meg, totally unaware.

How dare he?

Ellen looked down from the mirror, her eyes meeting Nick's eyes which were focused on hers. He gave her an inquisitive look before they both turned to watch Beth lift the cover of the box.

In the box lay a Victorian doll, an expensive one with a face made of fine porcelain. The dim light of the chandelier cast a ghostlike pall on the doll's complexion, emphasized by the drooping maroon velvet bonnet that framed her face and the matching coat that covered her, right up to her chin. The doll's eyes were closed tight. Metal fastenings bound her wrist and ankles to the support backing piece, holding her in place in the box.

Beth let go of the box. Meg caught it just before it fell to the floor. "That dolly looks sick, Mommy."

In a soothing tone, Meg said, "She's only sleeping, Beth. See how pretty she is?" Meg stood the box upright. The doll's eyes flew open. Beth screamed and reached for the elephant. Nick put his long arm around Beth and the elephant.

Flustered, Meg apologized. "I'm sorry, Julian. She's so very tired. It's way past her bedtime."

The muscles in Julian's neck tightened. "It's a collector's item, most likely just for display anyway. She'll like it in a few years."

After a moment of uncomfortable silence, Carl clapped his hands. "Time for the birthday games." Giving Meg a hug, he said, "Delicious dinner, hon."

Ellen glanced at the mirror and saw an expression on Julian's face that made her own face turn as white as the doll's pasty complexion. It wasn't love this time or anything close to it. A mask of hatred had appeared on Julian's face as he stared at Carl hugging Meg.

Carl moved away from Meg and left the room to bring back

the games. Julian again focused his gaze on Meg, long and soft, then averted his eyes when she turned. Time and again, he stared when she wasn't noticing. Meg, pouring soda. Meg, smoothing away cake crumbs. Meg, laughing and enjoying herself. Like a cat ready to pounce, he watched her every move.

You're not the least bit interested in this birthday, the dinner, or the company, Ellen thought. *There's only one reason you're here. My sister.* Like the pull of a magnet, Ellen couldn't stop looking at his reflection. Glancing up suddenly, his eyes locked with hers for what seemed to be an eternity.

Julian was the first to look away. He nudged her gently with his elbow. She looked away from the mirror and saw his face creased with tension. Holding out a plate, he asked, "Would you like some birthday cake, Ellen?"

Before Ellen could answer, Ruth said, "It's later than I thought. We'd love to stay longer, but there's a town meeting at eight, and we need to leave."

After their good-byes, Meg explained to Beth and Matthew that there would be only one game due to the late hour. "We're going to play pin the tail on the donkey," she said.

While Carl taped the poster of the donkey on the refrigerator, Meg put a blindfold on Beth and attached a piece of tape to the paper tail, then placed it in her right hand. Beth twirled around twice and headed away from the refrigerator, toward Ellen. Taking one hesitant step after another, Beth kept her hand outstretched. Her mouth was tightly closed.

"Good girl," teased Matthew in his big brother's voice. "You're going to win."

Beth smiled widely, revealing miniature dimples that looked vaguely familiar to Ellen. Ignoring the donkey tail that was aimed her way, Ellen leaned forward to get a closer look. When she saw the tiny indentations that resembled a star, Ellen dropped the glass of water in her hand, barely aware of the sounds of glass and ice cubes hitting the floor.

Startled by the noise, Beth dropped the tail and pulled down her blindfold. Confused that she wasn't facing the picture of a donkey, she stared at Ellen with bewildered, deep brown eyes. Ellen felt another jolt of recognition. Beth's eyes were similar to the eyes that had stared back at her in a different setting. Theresa's.

Beth ran toward Matthew. "You sent me the wrong way," she said, crying.

"You're a baby," Matthew said.

"Enough," said Carl, picking them up, Beth in one arm, Matthew in the other. "Let's go into the living room and calm down now."

Nick was staring at Ellen, with eyes that probed hers, searching for whatever it was that had startled her.

She bent down to pick up the water glass but couldn't get a grip on it because her hands were shaking.

Meg went into the pantry for paper towels.

"Let me help," said Julian, reaching down. An envelope fell out of his jacket pocket, landing just inches from the streaming liquid. Ellen put her hand out to prevent the envelope from getting wet.

Just as her hand touched the envelope, something hard came crushing down on the tips of her fingers. It was Julian's shoe.

Julian grabbed the envelope from under her hand. "I'm so sorry," he said. "Are you all right, Ellen?"

Stifling a cry of pain, Ellen took a piece of ice from the floor and held it to her fingers. Nick came around the table and knelt beside her. Taking her hand, he saw the red marks. Turning to Julian, he asked, "What just happened?"

Julian gave a dismissive laugh. "You must have learned by now that Ellen always manages to be in the wrong place at the wrong time. This time her hand got in the way of my size eleven."

Nick released Ellen's hands and stood, facing Julian, who was now on his feet. "You think that's funny?" Nick demanded.

For the first time, Ellen noticed that Julian and Nick were the same height. Julian, doughy and pale, Nick, slender and muscular. And Nick looked more than ready for a fight.

Ellen pulled at Nick's sleeve. "Let it go," said Ellen. "It's Beth's party. Please. I'm all right."

Carl came back to the kitchen, carrying Beth and Matthew. "They're both tired, hon," he said to Meg.

Kissing each child on the forehead, Meg said, "Let Daddy take you upstairs and get your pajamas on."

Carl smiled at everyone. "I guess the party's over," he said. Meg stepped closer to Carl and put her arms out, embracing all three. For a moment, Ellen put her worries away and smiled at Nick, who was holding fresh ice on her hand. "I'd say this family is very big on group hugs, wouldn't you agree?"

Whispering in her ear, Nick said, "I'm only interested in a single hug, from a single lady."

From the corner of her eye, Ellen saw that Julian's chair was empty. A blast of night air brushed across the back of her neck as the kitchen door opened and closed behind her. Julian had let himself out.

CHAPTER THIRTY-EIGHT

Wednesday, March 16

Harvey walked ever so slowly into Cedar's Funeral Home for Rose Flanagan's wake. While Julian had most of the funeral business in town, due to his established family name, Cedar's was a close second. His legs beginning to stiffen, Harvey couldn't kneel at the casket. He gripped his cane and bowed his head to view Rose Flanagan. He had seen Rose a few weeks before when he visited the Pomarium. He enjoyed playing board games with the residents, which whiled away the hours of his long days without Margaret. His aches and pains were minimal that day, and he had managed to get around to the kitchen to say hello to Rose. She had been the picture of health and had given Harvey a glass of water to take with his pills.

This makes three dead people in less than a week. Eric, Ed Lake, and Rose. I would have bet that the third would have been me.

Harvey turned and slowly made his way up the middle aisle. The visitors who went before him had already left. A middle-aged woman, sitting in the last row, nodded to him. He stopped short and leaned on his cane. He recognized Theresa from his visits to the Pomarium. She looked at him with deep brown eyes, which Margaret would have said had soul.

"Mr. Poston, I was planning to call you."

"And why would that be?" he asked kindly.

"Well, I was first going to call you about how to go about handling my father's estate. I don't know anything about those kinds of things."

"My dear, I'm retired, but I'll be glad to give you some guidance. Come see me tomorrow."

"But now there's something else." Theresa's face became radiant, exposing a deep dimple on her cheek. "If I tell you, will you please keep my confidence?"

"Why, yes, of course. I can direct you to the right attorney tomorrow. We can't talk here."

Excitement in her voice, she talked quickly, ignoring the hand Harvey put up as a signal to stop. "A wonderful miracle has happened. Many years ago, I had a baby that I thought had died, but now I know she is alive and well. I want to do things right by her."

The cane Harvey was leaning on suddenly didn't seem sturdy enough to support him. Clenching it even tighter, he raised his head slightly to peer through the lower part of his spectacles and studied her carefully. She didn't seem like the withdrawn girl who worked in the Pomarium kitchen. She was happy.

Harvey noticed a few people coming in the door. Lowering his voice, he said, "Before you say any more, we should go into one of the private rooms."

"Oh, no. There's so much I need to do."

"What you have just told me is a very serious matter, and perhaps a legal one. You must not repeat this to anyone else. Do not do anything until we talk. And whatever you do, promise me you won't contact the daughter who you think may be yours."

She abruptly rose from her seat and turned to go.

"Please, wait. It's best we talk, now," he said, beginning to wheeze. "Please, I ask you, don't go yet."

"I'll call you," she said, turning and walking quickly up the aisle.

And there was no way the wheezing, old lawyer holding tight to his cane with one hand, could catch up with her. All he could do was fumble, with his free hand, into his pocket for a handkerchief to dab at the tears welling up in his eyes.

After the service, driving home from Cedar's Funeral Home, Harvey turned his thoughts to an infant born twenty-five years ago, who had grown and matured not only into a beautiful woman but a contented one. Meg didn't know she was under Harvey's watchful eye, albeit from a distance. He couldn't afford to bring attention to himself. The price would have been too high.

A lot of good I am to anyone now, Harvey thought. Then his thoughts turned to the grandfather Meg never knew she had. "You fool, Ed Lake," he muttered. "It's too bad you didn't live long enough to see what you missed.

"Or what you could have prevented."

CHAPTER THIRTY-NINE

Wednesday, March 16

Nick sat beside Ellen on the couch in Meg's living room. Drawing in a sigh, he asked, "Why do I have feeling that I'll be driving back to Boston by myself tonight?"

When she didn't answer, he said, "I know something happened at the dining table. Your face turned white when Beth pointed the donkey's tail toward you. And all those silent looks between you and Julian? Come on, basic journalism: body language speaks louder than words. If you'd stop shutting me out, maybe I can help."

She took his hands in hers. "You can help me, Nick, by being understanding."

Nick shook his head. "You're still doing it," he said.

Ellen took a deep breath. "Okay, you're right. I have been shutting you out, but not because I don't trust you. It's just that there are a few leads I need to check, and it's not fair to say anything until I do. I promise I'll tell you about it as soon as I work some things out."

She wished she could tell him everything now, so he could tell her she was wrong, that her imagination was working overtime. But there was no mistaking what she had seen. Julian's obsession with her sister had been plain, and there was no question about the resemblance between Beth and Theresa. Each had star-like dimples that were revealed only by bright smiles. And they both had deep brown eyes that darkened like charcoal when they were afraid. Ellen needed time to think.

Remembering her abrupt manner the last time she had sent Nick back home alone, she began to apologize. "I was looking so forward to being with you alone tonight, but—."

He released her hands and put two of his fingers to her lips. "Say no more. Do what you need to do. I should get going. After all, someone has to mind the store." He got up from the couch and put his hand out to her, then drew her close when she stood.

"On a serious note," he said, "there's something going on at work. Rumor has it that there are big organizational changes and some management opportunities on the horizon. If you want to be in the running, you'd better get yourself back there."

"I just got a promotion," she said. "And I've barely had a chance to run the features department."

Nick grinned. "You know how our employer does things. And it won't be very satisfying if I get an upper-level job without some stiff competition."

She couldn't help smiling. "I'll be there, Nick Stanton. And you're the one who should watch out. Be forewarned."

Pressing her even closer to him, he murmured into her ear, "All that matters is that I love you, and I'm waiting for you to say you love me back."

Ellen felt a familiar stirring. That was definitely Nick's doing —a feeling he created inside her with more and more ease. She forced a laugh and said, "Get out of here." But instead of pushing him away, she tightened her arms around his neck. *Don't leave*, she wanted to say. *I'm so very afraid of what I might find out.*

Meg came to the doorway. Her face was flushed and her blue eyes were tearing. "I think I may be coming down with something, so I'll keep my distance. Have a safe trip." She touched her lips and blew them a kiss.

Ellen whispered to Nick. "She doesn't know I'm not going back to Boston."

"Allow me," Nick whispered.

"Dear Meg," he said, going over to her and putting his hand on the sleeve on her robe. "I want you to know you have my sympathy, first because you're under the weather and second, because you're stuck with this woman for another night."

The red splotches on Meg's face turned scarlet. "What? You're not going back?"

"I can explain," Ellen said.

Meg put her hands over her ears. "I don't want to hear it. Good night." She went into the hallway, narrowly missing Beth and Matthew who had bounded down the stairs.

Matthew ran up to Nick. "My birthday is in June. Will you come?"

"Sure," Nick replied, and Ellen could see he was touched.

Beth hugged Ellen, asking, "Auntie, when are you coming back to stay with us?" Ellen picked her niece up and rocked her, then, still holding her, drew back so she could study Beth's face. "I'm staying one more night, sweetie."

From the doorway, Nick said, "Hey, Beth, how about me? Aren't you going to invite me back?"

At the sound of his voice, Beth smiled as wide as a Jack-o-lantern. Ellen watched as the star-shaped dimple appeared. Beth nodded her head.

"I think the answer is yes," said Ellen, hugging Beth as tight as she could.

Oh, precious little one, she thought. *What if I'm right? What if you are the image of your maternal grandmother, Theresa Francis Lake?*

Thursday, March 17

Meg had woken up with a fever. Ellen assured Carl she would take care of everything—Meg, the children, the chores, the meals.

"You have no idea how much this helps," Carl said. "I had to let my assistant manager go. My payroll is so stretched. I need to be at work."

"It's okay," Ellen said. "We're family, and this is what we do."

One hour later, wearing a flannel shirt and blue jeans that belonged to Meg, Ellen pushed a bundle of clothes into the washing machine.

Carl had taken Matthew to school, and Ellen had Beth ready to be picked up by Aunt Ruth, who was bringing her to her house for the day. She hadn't had time to think about the unthinkable: how could Meg possibly be the daughter of Eric and Theresa? And if she was, how was it that Ellen and Eric's parents wound up raising Meg as their daughter?

Ellen couldn't imagine Chief Lake allowing such an arrangement with the parents of the young man he hated. After all, he was convinced that Eric had ruined his daughter.

Ellen thought about the lengths her parents must have gone to in order to raise the baby as their own. All those years, in this small town, they'd carried out a deception. But Ellen had seen her mother's pregnancy with her own eyes. She remembered the day she went to the hospital, and the morning, a few days later, when her mother and father brought the baby home. Ellen was sure it was in April. She remembered making Easter cutouts while she waited in the hardware store after school so her father could look after her. And the lilac trees were getting ready to bloom. They always celebrated Meg's birthday in April. But Rose said Theresa's baby was born in March.

Ellen picked up a sock that had fallen to the floor, opened the lid of the washer, and watched the agitator come to a stop. She dropped the sock into the sudsy water, then closed the cover and listened while the agitator restarted its cycle. *Everything that goes around comes around.* Harvey's words.

Was it a coincidence that Theresa and Esther gave birth to daughters about the same time? Her mother was over forty when Meg was born.

The washing machine began its final rinse cycle, and Ellen realized that she had been standing there for a long time, her thoughts whirling. She put the clothes in the dryer and tried to pin down her ideas. She had to get to Theresa, but where was she?

Maybe she should just tell her sister what she suspected. But Meg was sick. She recalled the expression on Julian's face the night before. His look of obsession gave her chills. She would find answers today, even if she had to retrace all of her steps. She was getting good at that.

Her plan began to take shape. First, she would go to the old age home to try again to talk to Brother Lester. Then she would visit Harvey to see if the kindly lawyer could remember anything more. And finally, she thought, she would visit Julian and demand to see Eric's letter. *And if all of this gets me nowhere, then I'll have no recourse but to tell Meg about my suspicions. Maybe even as soon as tonight.*

Ellen put her mind on the domestic duties of the morning, the list of which seemed endless. She arranged a tray of juice and toast and brought it upstairs. Finding Meg sound asleep, she left the tray on the night table and went into Matthew's bedroom where she made his bed and gathered clothes for the second load of wash. When she was leaving the room, she noticed a picture of Matthew and Carl taken at a baseball game, reminding her of Nick with the children during the birthday party.

Nick, author of a children's book, was meant to be a father one day. She was heady with the thought of an intimate relationship with Nick. Would it be clandestine or bold and daring? Either way, the anticipation was unbearable. And what did it matter if people knew? After all, they lived in Boston, not Springton. She still could hardly believe that an act of passion twenty-five years ago had caused the banishment of two young people—

and resulted in secrets decades old, intended to be buried with the dead.

She scooped up the dirty laundry and carried it down the stairs. When the telephone rang, she picked up the receiver on the first ring so it wouldn't awaken Meg.

"Is this Ellen Von Der Hyde?" a raspy voice asked on the other end of the line.

"Yes, it is."

"I thought for sure I'd hear from you by now, the way you were trying to put two and two together."

"Harvey!" she said. "You were second on my list of people to visit this afternoon."

"In that case, I suggest that you make me the first," he said. "Before it's too late."

CHAPTER FORTY

The hallway in Harvey's house was as cold as the outdoors. Ellen followed him to the closed kitchen door. When he opened it, she was brushed by a rush of warm air from a space heater.

Seeing her concern, Harvey said, "Don't worry, that heater is only temporary. Ruth Anderson came by this morning, and when she realized the heating problem ... well, it was kind of hard to hide ... she called her furnace serviceman. He'll be out this afternoon." He gave Ellen a knowing look. "I suppose all this is just a happy coincidence."

Grinning at the thought of Ruth taking immediate action, Ellen changed the subject. "You sound much better than you did on the telephone this morning." She took off her coat and put it on a rocking chair next to the stove.

"Thanks to my trusty inhaler," he answered, gesturing for her to sit in one of two ladder-back chairs at the wobbly farm table. He brought over two jars of jelly and set them next to a plate of biscuits. Squinting, Harvey read the labels. "Both the same," he said, "What is your preference, apple or apple?"

Ellen laughed. "Either one is fine with me."

He put one of the jars in front of her. "You can open this faster than I."

With a slight twist, Ellen opened the lid of the jelly jar. The sweet aroma reminded Ellen of autumn leaves. So different from the sour jelly Theresa had found.

"Oh, I almost forgot. I brought you a piece of birthday cake," Ellen said, reaching into her bag and taking out a triangular piece of cake wrapped in waxed paper. She set it on the table.

Harvey nodded. "Meg's birthday cake," he said, almost to himself.

The implication of his words didn't escape her. Bracing herself for what might come next, she said, "No, it's Meg's daughter's birthday. Beth will be four next week."

Harvey put down his glass. "It's Meg's birthday," he said firmly.

Ellen put the lid back on the jar and fingered the label, a replica of parchment with calligraphy in amber ink.

"All right, let's get down to business," Harvey said. "I saw Theresa Lake at calling hours for Rose. Interesting, that it wasn't held at the Baker Funeral Home."

He leaned closer to Ellen. "Young lady, it is my hope that you have figured it out by now. And if you haven't, I'm disappointed in you. Things are coming around again. We're talking about identity, that maybe things aren't what they seem to be. Do you follow me?"

"I know what my parents did if that's what you mean. They raised Theresa and Eric's baby, who is Meg, as their own child. But what I can't figure out is how they got Chief Lake to go along with it."

Harvey shook his head. "Ed Lake didn't go along with a damn thing." He sighed. "This is a story I didn't think would be mine to tell. So I might as well start at the beginning: "Once upon a time, there was a doctor, a lawyer, and ... " His voice trailed off.

Ellen filled in the missing words. "And a police chief," she said, pushing away a fleeting thought that maybe she wasn't ready to hear what was to come. *But it's now or never*, she thought, taking a deep breath. She had come too far to go back. Ellen settled back in her chair, prepared to let Harvey's words play out in her mind's eye, as if she were watching a reel of film.

It was in November when Chief Edwin Lake strode into Harvey's office, with no notice. There was a razor-sharp edge to his voice when he said, 'I've taken my daughter to work at the monastery, Harv. She'll live with Rose, the cook, in a separate building there. Theresa's pregnant, and it's too late to have it fixed.'

'Is there anything I can do?' Harvey asked, knowing full well the answer would be yes.

After the chief told him of his plans, Harvey asked him to reconsider. 'There has to be another way,' he said. 'You just don't tell a mother her baby is dead and then whisk it away for strangers to adopt, Ed. It's a heartless thing for a man to do to his own daughter.'

Nothing he said budged the chief. Everything was arranged. He had brought Theresa to Doc Sutton, who determined that the baby was due in mid-March. To keep the birth quiet, the delivery would take place in the doctor's home, which housed his office. Lucy, the doctor's wife who also was his nurse, would assist him. Theresa would be given anesthesia and told her baby was stillborn. There was no need for her to know that it was going to be adopted. The chief insisted that no one else should know. There had been enough town gossip about his wife and older daughter Victoria. He couldn't take any more.

'And you want me draw up adoption papers, is that it, Ed?' the lawyer asked.

'More than that, Harvey. I want you to find a couple to adopt the baby. It's got to be someone out of town. Keep the Lake name out of it. Theresa's middle name is Francis. Use Francis for the last name on the papers.'

'I'll make some calls,' he said reluctantly, 'but there's no guarantee. The laws are getting tougher every year on things like this. I'll see what I can find out.'

'You do that, Harvey. But there's one more thing. You're wrong about

there being no guarantee. That is, if you and Margaret value your impeccable reputations in this town.'

Harvey feigned calmness. He wanted to say, 'Don't you see, you're running out of people who care about you? You fool, you'll have nothing left but your bottle.'

Instead, he said, 'If you don't mind my asking, what does the father of the child say about this plan?'

Ed Lake's lips formed a thin sneer. 'Let's just say, if you knew who the father is, maybe you'd be a little more understanding.' He stormed out of the office and slammed the door behind him.

When Harvey heard the screech of tires, he knew the police chief of Springton was on his way home to his liquor cabinet.

Within hours, a colleague in Boston said he could put Harvey in touch with a couple desperately wanting a baby. There would be no questions. Harvey was appalled, mostly at himself.

There had to be another way. He would talk to Margaret.

Margaret listened, her clenched jaw and folded arms a sure sign of her fury. Harvey's wife of thirty years had come from a long line of independent females. He never knew her to make a bad judgment call. More than once he thought she would have made the better lawyer. She had no tolerance for injustice and overcame her despair at not being able to bear children by throwing herself into every community activity possible.

When he finished, her words stunned him. 'I already know about the Lake girl's pregnancy. Lucy Sutton told me while we were setting up for Red Cross training courses.'

Harvey couldn't believe he heard right. 'What in the world did she tell you?'

'She said that when Theresa came in for her examination, the girl had blurted out that the father was Eric Von Der Hyde.' Margaret shook her head. 'The poor thing had so much grief inside in her heart that it had to come out, whether she meant it to or not.'

Margaret brushed him off when he said he needed time to formulate a plan. 'It's already done,' she said. 'Esther and Rudolph reacted just the way I thought they would.'

'You told them?' he asked in disbelief.

'Of course. They're coming here tomorrow to see what possible recourse they have.'

She softened toward Harvey only when he agreed to her plan. 'You're right, Margaret. There's an innocent baby with a bloodline to a family here. I'm willing to cross Chief Lake.' He told himself that if she could go through with it, so would he. Then he prepared himself for the meeting as best as he could.

A stoic couple, Esther and Rudolph didn't flinch when Harvey told them that adoptive parents had been located.

Esther spoke first. 'As we told Margaret, there's no need for one of our own to be brought up by strangers. We want to bring the baby up as our own son or daughter.'

Rudolph's eyes bored into Harvey's. 'My wife is being very polite. What we mean is that if there is nothing we can do to change Lake's mind to let Theresa keep the infant, then we will take matters into our own hands. We're not afraid of any scandal. And don't think I'm afraid of Lake either.'

Esther nodded in agreement.

'Well, you should be afraid,' Harvey said. 'Let's not forget that Ed's hatred goes back much further than this. Even before your son met Theresa.'

Rudolph waved away the suggestion. 'That's water under the bridge. I can't imagine Lake thinks about that anymore.' He put his arm protectively around Esther's shoulder.

'Don't you? Ed Lake never gives up a grudge. Can't you see he's already established power over you by forcing you to send Eric away? And now I know why you came in here a few months back to change your wills. Leaving your estate to that church in Keaton? It's called blackmail. And if that's not enough, wait until the next time he's drunk. You're in for big trouble if this isn't done right.'

Esther turned to her husband. 'Harvey's right, dear,' she said softly. 'We have no choice but to follow Margaret's plan. Thank you, Harvey, for agreeing to this. We wouldn't be able to do it without you.'

Margaret looked at Harvey with pride. She was confident her plan would work out. The baby would not be whisked away to strangers. Margaret would help Esther fake her own pregnancy. The two women squeezed each other's hands.

Harvey didn't mention that if the plan failed and Lake found out that Harvey and his wife were conspiring with Esther and Rudolph Von Der Hyde, he could kiss his career good-bye. Lake would see to it that his legal practice went down in flames.

Harvey now lapsed into silence, leaving Ellen to wonder if he was lost in his own memories or if he decided he had said enough. Worried that it might be the latter, she urged him to go on. "You referred to other things that happened in the past. What were they?"

He took off his glasses and wiped them with a paper napkin, then put them on again. "Back before your parents were married, Ed Lake had a crush on your mother. She was a beautiful girl. Lake was a handsome young man. Esther was the only girl in Springton he couldn't get."

Ellen shook her head. "This is incredible."

"Esther only dated one boy. Your father. Rudolph was plain but reliable, not a handsome basketball star, like Lake, who was cocky enough to think that when he became a policeman, he'd get the girl. Well, big surprise. Esther married Rudolph, and Ed took a lot of razzing. As you can imagine, when Rudolph's son dared to fall for his daughter and got her pregnant, there was bad blood on Ed's part. And Ed had a plan to make your parents pay dearly. He intimidated them enough to change their wills."

With a glance at the empty rocking chair, Harvey said, "But Esther and Rudolph received something in return that was worth more than any amount of money ... they got to raise a beautiful baby." He turned his gaze on Ellen and went silent.

"Harvey?" Ellen asked gently. "Are you able to continue?"

He nodded. "There's no turning back on this road."

My sentiments exactly, thought Ellen.

Like clockwork, the labor pains began the day the baby was due. Theresa was taken to the Sutton's house.

The baby came fast, just as Theresa was put under with anesthesia. Theresa was healthy, and the delivery was as uncomplicated as the nine months leading up to it. Doc Sutton and his wife gave the perfect six-pound girl every bit of care she would have received had she been born in a hospital.

There was a half-moon that night and about eight o'clock, a car pulled around to the back of the house. The driver got out and opened the back door of the car and the doctor put the bundled-up newborn into a sturdy basket. The driver followed his instructions to the letter and headed to Boston. Only when he was certain that he wasn't being followed, the driver took a sharp turn on a secondary road. He drove to a large white house about two miles away from the Sutton place, drove around to the back, and flicked his headlights twice.

The lights in the kitchen and back porch went on, and Lucy Sutton hurried out, with Margaret watching from the doorway. Lucy took the basket with the sleeping baby from the back seat and carried it into the house. The porch light went off.

The driver left without a word and took the car back to the rental agency in the next town. He returned to Springton by bus, then picked up his own car at the bus station. When he got home in the early hours of the morning, he walked into the kitchen and witnessed a beautiful sight. Margaret was sitting in a rocker and feeding a bottle of formula to a baby wrapped in a pink blanket, with Lucy watching over them, an approving smile on her face.

Ellen could hardly catch her breath. "And you were the driver, Harv," Ellen whispered. She glanced at the rocking chair. "This is the kitchen."

"I can see them now," he said, his eyes glassing over. "Margaret, a tad nervous, Lucy hovering over her like a mother hen." He smiled. "My wife had never taken care of an infant before, but she did a fine job, for about four weeks."

Ellen gasped. "Meg was here for all that time?" His voice faltering, Harvey said, "Please get my pills next to the sugar bowl on the counter. Two pinks and a white. There's not much time."

Alarmed, Ellen gave him the pills and a glass of water, which he took with shaking hands. Trying not to panic, she asked, "Should I call your doctor?"

With a weak laugh, he said, "I don't mean I'm going to die today. I'm not ready to let that undertaker get my bones. Now, where was I? Yes, I remember. We had Meg for the first four weeks of her life. That was part of Margaret's scheme. Then, one night in April, we discretely brought the baby to live with your parents. And we let it be known around town, gradually, that your mother had given birth to her third child."

"But there's one part of this I can't understand."

"Which would be what?"

"It would have been impossible for my mother to fake a pregnancy."

"Oh, you think?"

"Then tell me how."

"We carried out this plan in the month of December. The winter was very cold, with a couple of blizzards, and your parents lived on a remote road, a dead-end lane. So they weren't exactly town fixtures. Esther only needed to wear a heavy coat if she made an appearance in town. She may even have strapped a pillow to her abdomen. From December on, your mother looked pregnant. Seemed a natural time to begin showing.

"And during the last month of the pregnancy, my dear wife Margaret and her friend Lucy Sutton were so protective that if anyone asked about Esther, they made it clear Esther was on complete bedrest. So, in April it simply seemed Esther had given birth to a healthy baby. Lots of women gave birth at home in those days." Harvey peered at Ellen through his glasses. "So now you know how it was done. I hope you're all right with it."

Ellen wasn't sure how she felt about all these revelations, but she knew that wasn't the point. "It doesn't matter about me," she told Harvey. "It's how Meg will take it."

ॐ

After Harvey saw Ellen to the door, he cursed his lawyer's ethics that stopped him from mentioning his conversation with Theresa. He had assured Theresa that what she told him was in confidence. He had bent the law once when he drew up fake adoption papers, convincing himself it was the only way that Meg could be raised in her own family and not by strangers, as Lake intended. But Theresa hadn't mentioned Meg by name, and he had asked her not to do anything until she met with him. Harvey had no right to meddle in that girl's life again.

Oh, Margaret, he thought, *what would you say to all this?*

CHAPTER FORTY-ONE

Thursday, March 17

The harsh ring of the doorbell pulled Meg from a deep sleep. She noticed the toast and juice on the night table and then glanced at the porcelain clock that had belonged to Carl's mother.

She'd been asleep for hours. The last thing she remembered was hearing the sounds of household activity, the distant hum of the dryer, bowls being stacked in cupboards. Despite her fever and aching head and bones, she smiled at how domestic Ellen had been that morning. She had even arranged for Aunt Ruth to take care of Beth for the day.

The doorbell rang again, jangling the pain in her head. *It's time to have the old thing replaced*, Meg thought, *one more expense*. She put on her robe and slippers.

Holding on to the handrail, she made it down the stairs. She opened the door and faced a woman who stared at her in silence. The salt-and-pepper hair that fell beneath a coarsely knitted hat framed a heart-shaped face with deep-set brown eyes and a pug nose that must have been cute when the woman was younger. Meg recognized Theresa Lake immediately. The likeness of Ellen's sketch was remarkable.

"I know who you are, Theresa," she said. "Ellen has been looking all over for you. But please come back later. I'm sick."

Unblinking, Theresa seemed to hear only the last sentence. "I can tell you're ill, my poor darling." Briefly, she touched Meg's cheek with a cool hand.

Meg, startled by the cold sensation on her cheek and the intensity of the woman's gaze, drew back, her hand still on the doorknob. "It's best if you keep your distance," she said. "Whatever I have may be contagious. Come back later." Noticing the stricken look on the woman's face, Meg added, "Please."

"Kindly let me in now, dear," urged Theresa. "I'll make you a cup of tea and take care of you."

The women kept their eyes on one another. Meg looked away first, feeling a surge of resentment. She wanted to scold Theresa for leaving Ellen alone in Chief Lake's house, for making their investigation so difficult, and for intruding in their lives. But there was something, an aura she couldn't identify, about the woman that silenced her.

A car door slammed, drawing Meg's attention away from the woman. Beth ran into the house and straight to the front closet. Aunt Ruth waved from the car, and Meg weakly waved back.

"I need my helmet. Auntie Ruth is taking me for a bike ride in the park."

"Is this your daughter?" Theresa asked, taking her eyes off Meg.

Meg instinctively put both hands on Beth's shoulders.

"Hello, I'm Theresa Lake," the woman said to Beth.

Beth, clutching her helmet, gave Theresa a wide smile and then broke away from Meg's grip and ran back to her aunt's car.

Meg's head was pounding, and she was wracked with chills. "I have a terrible headache," she said. "Please come back when Ellen is here."

Theresa looked at her with tenderness. "I never had the

chance to take care of my little baby. I wish you would let me take care of you now."

Meg didn't know what the woman was talking about and was too feverish to care. All she wanted was to go back to bed. "Listen," she said, "I don't know anything about a baby. I'm sorry, but you need to leave. Good-bye."

Theresa stepped back and then stood on the porch, still facing her.

Her strength drained, Meg slowly pushed the door shut and leaned against it, wondering if she could make it back up the stairs.

Ellen sat silently, thinking over all that Harvey had told her. For his part, the elderly lawyer seemed to have gained new energy in the telling of his story. He put a kettle on the stove and then tended to Piper, giving the dog a handful of treats. The dog had settled under the table near Ellen's feet.

Ellen reached down and patted the dog. She stood and walked to the window. Parting the faded cotton print curtains, she looked out at the sagging porch and imagined a half-moon night when an infant had been smuggled into this house.

She turned to face Harvey. "My poor brother. He didn't learn the whole story until he came back for our parents' funeral four years ago. And then when he did, he couldn't tell anyone, because of the chief. He must have been beside himself."

Harvey nodded, sadness crossing his face. "Remember, Eric was a man whose parents died tragically in an auto accident and who just found out they gave away their estate to a church they had never even attended. And then he discovers that his first love has spent the best years of her life in a monastery, all because of a pregnancy that he caused. Even worse, that Theresa thinks their baby was dead and buried in the very grave where the earth is still fresh after he buried his parents. And he's figured out that his parents raised the baby as their own. It's a bit much, even for an army officer, don't you think?"

The old lawyer continued. "When he came to see me again, he was as upset as I've ever seen a young man. I poured both of us a nip of brandy, something I just use for medicinal purposes, mind you. When he calmed down a bit, I told him the story I just told you. I couldn't bear to see that young man, who was serving our country, go so far away again with no answers. He was heartsick, I tell you."

"I'm sure," Ellen said. She watched Harvey as he took the kettle off the burner and took a tin of tea bags from a shelf. "You understand that when Meg finds out about all of this, nothing will ever be the same for her again."

Harvey sighed. "Eric had every intention of telling Meg. It was only a question of when. But what was the sense when he was returning to Europe to complete his tour of duty? Think about it. Meg was having a difficult pregnancy with Beth, and was sick, to say nothing of losing both her parents. And no one could predict Lake's reaction. He was as unpredictable as a spring snowstorm. I'm convinced that Eric planned to wait until his tour was over to make things as right as possible with Theresa and with Meg ... and to deal with Ed Lake."

CHAPTER FORTY-THREE

Thursday, March 17

The sharp architectural lines of the Victorian-style home that housed the Baker Funeral Home formed a looming silhouette against the grayness of a late winter morning.

Glancing at her watch, Ellen walked quickly up the steps and pressed long and hard on the doorbell. At the sound of the buzzer, she opened the door and stepped into the massive foyer. To her left, Julian sat facing her from behind a desk. A stack of wood was burning in the fireplace.

"What can I do for you?" he asked stiffly, not getting up.

Ellen crossed the polished hard wood floor. "I want to know what Eric said to you at the hospital."

"That's a strange question, Ellen. You know he was on his deathbed. The man couldn't talk. He gave me written instructions, which you have read."

"Is that all he gave you?"

Julian's eyes narrowed. "I resent this line of questioning."

"Is that so?" Ellen snapped. "Well, I resent your secrecy. You've watched me try to piece together things without lifting a finger to help. In fact, you've gotten in the way."

Ellen suddenly remembered what her ex had told her. Marty

Smith wouldn't have put nails in tires; he'd only wanted to scare her, not do any real harm. She had never suspected Julian. "You're the one who put nails in Meg's tires," Ellen said, her voice rising. "How clever, to do it at the cemetery, when Meg asked you for a ride home and you knew I'd be driving her car."

"Yes," he said calmly. "And when I came back to the house for lunch that day, I was disappointed to see you had made it back without a mishap. You don't belong here. Go back to Boston." Picking up a pen, he began to write.

Ellen slapped the desktop, harder than she meant to. He looked up, annoyance creasing his face. Lowering her voice and not taking her eyes off him, she said, "It's you who doesn't belong. Don't tell me there wasn't more to your visit with Eric. He had unfinished business."

Julian put the pen down. "It took you long enough to figure things out. Guess you're not as quick and smart as you think you are."

"I don't like deceit, Julian. I don't appreciate your going to Meg's house under the guise of being a family friend. You're obsessed with her and what's more, I think you're waiting to make your move. She loves Carl. They have a wonderful marriage. You're wasting your time."

"Don't think for one minute they always get along. There's been more than one time when I've come to the front door and overheard some of their squabbles."

"I wouldn't be too proud of eavesdropping, Julian. What I'm saying is that you're wasting your time."

Julian clasped his hands. "Time, you say. There are some things in life that are worth waiting for. And Meg is one of them. She is the essence of womanhood, beautiful and wholesome, filled with grace and serenity, and she's wasting her life on that bumpkin she's married to. Every day I think of her, living in that old house that's falling apart, cooking and slaving, I could ... well, it won't be long," he said, almost to himself. "I assure you, it won't be long."

Opening a top drawer, he took out a packet. "There are two envelopes in here," he went on. "One is addressed to me. In it is the letter that Meg read to you over the phone." He tossed it on the desk. Picking up the other, he held it out like a trophy. "This one is a heartfelt letter written to Meg from Eric, her long-lost father, which tells all." Gloating, he waved it.

"What a despicable thing for you to do. How dare you?" Ellen cried out.

"This is for me to give to Meg at the right time. When I'm ready."

At Ellen's incredulous look, he said, "Yes, she will come to me. Because one way or another, her marriage will be over and she will need me. Her children will need me. I will claim them as my own. They will have everything that Carl can't ever give them. This is my family."

Ellen was about to demand he give her the letter when a horrifying thought streaked across her mind. *Carl.*

Oh, God, no, she thought, taking a step back. "I'll leave," she said, turning around.

Julian said, "Good."

Her palms sweating, she got to the heavy door and grabbed the doorknob. With a sigh of relief, she felt it turn easily. She turned and saw Julian putting the letters in his drawer.

He looked up. "You've got nothing on me," he said. "No one will believe a word out of your mouth, especially considering the foolish way you've been behaving. Like prying into poor Rose Flanagan's past."

Ellen just stared at him, nearly paralyzed by a sudden realization. *My God, he may have killed Rose. Rose said she had suspicions about who Theresa's family was and would tell me if Theresa didn't come back. And Julian wants to control every bit of information that might matter to Meg.*

Ellen knew Julian was repulsive and had a creepy obsession

with her sister, but only now was she beginning to see that he was dangerous. *He's planning to kill Carl.*

"You're a coward," she said, the words coming out of her mouth before she could stop them.

She turned to grab the doorknob again but stopped cold at the sound of a click behind her, a sound that she recognized only because of the gangster movies she had seen. *The click of a hammer being pulled back on a handgun.*

"Poor choice of words, Ellen," he said, standing and coming around the desk. I haven't been called a coward since high school when I needed your big brother to save me. You should be acting like a sister to me instead of trying to ruin my life. You brought this all on yourself."

"None of what I do is any of your business," said Ellen, glancing around the room. *She had to get out. How?* She saw a foot-high bronze statuette on a mahogany drum table in front of one of the bay windows. Trying to look calm, she inched her way toward the table. It would be easy to smash one of the windowpanes with the statuette.

His voice stopped her from making another move. "Don't even think about it," he said, coming closer. "Get over here," he ordered, the handgun aimed at her face. "Now."

It seemed it took a lifetime for her to walk across the room. She had never seen a real gun. It gleamed, menacing, as if the opening on the barrel might swallow her into it. The hand that gripped it was steady. She was terrified. *Talk,* she thought. *Say something.*

"Julian," she began, "why are you doing this? Look, maybe I shouldn't have come barging in here, and maybe I said some things that may have seemed unfair. But I was upset."

"Don't beg, Ellen. It doesn't become you."

"What are you going to do?" She heard a tremor in her voice, and she was sure he heard it, too.

"Well, for starters, you can pick out your own casket. There are some very nice selections in the basement. On second thought, never mind, because you are going to disappear and you won't need one where you're going. But we'll have a nice memorial service for you. So, thanks. You have helped me a great deal. She'll need me sooner than I thought."

Ellen took a deep breath. "Tell me one thing, Julian. When did you decide you wanted Meg?"

"My love for Meg began four years ago, when your parents died, and Eric asked me to be there for her."

"He trusted you and you betrayed him."

For the first time, Julian's hand shook.

Ellen moved slightly to the right.

His hand steadied. He directed the gun at her.

She stood still.

Julian appeared to be talking to himself. "Eric saved my skin so many times. I loved and hated it at the same time. It was embarrassing to be a weakling. The King brothers would have kept hassling me if it weren't for Eric defending me.

"And then he went and got into trouble, with the police chief's daughter, no less, and sent away. I lost the only friend I ever had. But now I'm gaining something even better. Meg."

Ellen moved ever so slightly. If she could get back to the side of the desk, maybe she could make it to a window next to the fireplace. Nothing she had said had worked, and right now she would say anything. "I'm beginning to understand your feelings," she lied. "We both care about Meg and want what's best for her. We can work together, get beyond this, and try to be friends."

"I don't want a friend. I want Meg. It will be like having part of Eric back. I hated it when Eric went away. I want children. Meg's children. And not you or anyone else is going to stand in my way."

Julian pressed the gun into Ellen's back. "If you had minded your own business, this wouldn't be happening. Now do what I say. Walk to the basement door." He smiled at her. "I do believe you remember where it is."

When she didn't move, he ran the gun down her spine, the end of its barrel scraping against her vertebrae.

Grimacing from the pain radiating from her shoulders to her ribs, she inched to the door, with Julian so close behind she could feel his breath on her neck. They walked as one, their shadows against the wall of the corridor playing a grotesque pattern, a two-headed being making its way to what could be her death. Would Julian really kill her? she wondered. Was he that obsessed with Meg?

He nudged her down the stairs into a dark room on the left. With the gun still at her back, he pushed the light switch on with his free hand, then shoved her into a desk chair and locked the door behind them.

Squinting while she adjusted her eyes to the brightness of the overhead light, Ellen realized she was staring into her sister's eyes. Taking up half a wall in front of her was a blown-up photo of Meg, standing on the beach, laughing. A huge wave loomed in the background. The dampness of her white chambray dress made it cling to her body, its translucency revealing a white two-piece bathing suit underneath. Her skin was as tan as the wet sand she stood in, her smile radiant.

This is one of her honeymoon photos, Ellen thought. Julian had said he knew the house better than she did. She could just picture him slipping the photo from the album when no one was looking.

She was just beginning to understand the lengths that Julian would go to get Meg. And it terrified her. *I've got to do something,* she thought. *I've got to save Meg.*

Ellen stood, as if to look more closely at the photos, and as she did Julian grabbed her arm, twisted it, then shoved her back into the chair. "Don't do that again," he told her.

She turned her head so he wouldn't see the tears welling up from the pain—and faced more pictures of Meg. Blinking hard, trying to will the tears not to fall, Ellen concentrated on the collage of photos on the wall. Behind her, Julian opened and slammed drawers. Not seeming to find what he wanted, he cursed.

The collection seemed to be endless. In one photo Meg stood, being presented a blue ribbon by a judge, an oversized pie on the table in front of them. Another showed Meg decorating a Christmas tree, a white angel in one hand while she stood on the top rung of a ladder. Part of the photo was torn away.

Trying not to think of what Julian might be looking for, Ellen noticed that a strong hand gripped the ladder in the photo. Carl's hand. It was Carl who had been ripped out of the picture. Ellen realized that many of the photos were torn in half.

You've already killed Carl in your mind, she thought.

From the corner of her eye, Ellen thought she saw something move. Turning, all she saw was a smudged basement-sized window pane, and beneath it, a black-and-white photo that she recognized. It was Meg, sitting on their parents' front porch swing, her arm around what had been the shoulders of a person now cut out of the photo. Branches of lilacs were on Meg's lap. Rudolph had taken the picture of Meg and Ellen during the lilac season, when the girls helped him prune the trees. And Ellen, like Carl, had been cut out of the picture.

Again, she thought she saw movement. Looking up at the window, she saw a man's shoe that quickly disappeared.

Someone was outside. Help might be on the way.

"What was that?" Julian demanded.

"What was what?"

"Whatever made you look up at the window."

"Nothing made me look up," Ellen lied.

He moved in front of her, his left hand holding a syringe and a vial. The gun was in his right hand. Putting the syringe and vial on top of the table, he opened the drawer. "Ah, there it is, right on top," he said, pulling out a strip of rubber tubing.

She felt her heart racing. Was he planning to poison her?

Slamming the drawer shut, he faced Ellen triumphantly. "I thank you again, Ellen. If you hadn't come along I would still be biding my time, playing the part of a hanger on, waiting for the right moment. Remember, Eric and I used to play games. For the first time, I'm the winner, and Meg is my prize."

Julian put the gun in his pocket. He inserted the needle into the vial, held it to the light, and slowly extracted the blue contents into it, then nodded with satisfaction. "What's that saying? 'This will hurt you more than me'?"

A faint sound came from upstairs. Ellen knew she had to buy time. She had to keep him talking. Ignoring the pain, she said, "I've never seen some of these photos of Meg. Tell me, do you have the one where she was on that float in the parade when she was named Miss Community Achiever?"

He snorted. "That picture wasn't worth the paper it was printed on. Why, you couldn't even see Meggie, she was so hidden behind all those flowers."

Meggie, thought Ellen miserably. *She had never been called Meggie in her life. He was even renaming her.*

Watching Julian as he came to stand in front of her, the syringe poised as if he were holding a knife, Ellen kept talking. "Please, tell me your favorite picture. Is it the one at the ocean?"

"Wrong," he said with a smile. "That's only my second favorite." He spun her chair around and ripped a cloth off the wall. "That's my favorite."

Ellen gasped at the portrait of Meg. This was no photo. Rather, it was a large oil painting in an elaborate gold frame.

It must be one of the paintings that Julian had said wasn't for public viewing, she thought. In soft brush strokes, the artist had used pastels to dress Meg in a low-cut chiffon dress. Lilacs spilling out of a crystal vase on a pedestal table beside her complemented the soft pastel hues of the dress and highlighted the glow of Meg's complexion.

But it was the oversized ring gleaming from her sister's ring finger that caught Ellen's attention. It lent a garish detail against the softness of the portrait which, she had to reluctantly admit, was a well-done likeness of Meg.

Noticing Ellen's gaze, Julian said proudly, "That was my mother's ring. The band is 22-karat gold, the stone five carats. The first thing I'm going to do is to throw away that dime-store ring Meggie's wearing now. He ran his fingers caressingly along the outline of the woman in the portrait. "Meggie deserves so much more," he whispered. "I'll make sure she gets it."

Again, Ellen thought she heard noises. She had to take advantage of Julian's distraction. "Who's the artist?" she asked.

"Who else but me? I did it from memory. It's going to be my wedding gift to my bride. This portrait will hang in our bedroom." He turned the chair around and then moved toward her with the tubing.

Ellen tried not to flinch. Raising her voice, she said, "There's something wrong with this portrait."

"What do you mean?"

"Meg doesn't look happy, Julian. She looks trapped, miserable. No, it's worse than that. There's hatred on her face. Yes, that's it. She hates that ugly ring. Almost as much as she has grown to hate you."

He towered over her. "How dare you say that Meggie will hate the ring that my mother wore? How dare you say that she will come to hate me? She'll worship the ground I walk on. It's too bad you won't be around to see it happen.

"And who are you to tell me she looks unhappy? I painted Meggie to be the epitome of a loved woman, a picture of the contentment that is brought out by the love of one man. And I'm the only man who can give her that kind of love."

Ellen gave a derisive laugh. "You painted nothing but a mockery of Meg. It's obscene and degrading. It's an epitome, all right. The epitome of bad taste. But I'll give you this much. You painted a picture of a woman who will have nothing but contempt for you forever. If *you* knew the first thing about my sister, you'd realize she's in love with the man she married." As soon as the words were out, Ellen knew she had just pushed this obsessed man too far.

Julian turned to her slowly. "Get up," he said, dropping the syringe and taking the gun from his pocket. "You won't die the humane way, like Rose did. That's much too good for you." He unlocked the door. "Go back up the stairs and take a left at the top. We are going to walk to the end of the hall where there is an empty casket."

So he did murder Rose, Ellen thought, terror coursing through her body. She tried not to tremble as she got up from the chair, listening for any kind of activity from upstairs. There was only silence. *Was she wrong? Had it only been a pedestrian walking by?* She felt faint as she obediently walked up the stairs, with Julian behind her, his gun boring into her waist.

In a tired voice, Julian said, "You're very fortunate, Ellen. How many people do you think get the chance to see their own casket? You'll like this one. It's a model my penny-pinching father picked up at a closeout sale years ago. And you won't even have to pay for it. By the way, it has pink cushions. It'll look awful with your coloring."

Ellen made it to the top of the stairs and into the hallway. She took a step to the right and looked across the foyer to the locked front door. *There must be a side door,* she thought desperately.

"I said, turn left," said Julian, poking her with the gun. Suddenly, a uniformed policeman appeared in the doorway of the foyer. A thin stream of light danced eerily from his badge to the gun he pointed at them. His face was in the shadows, but Ellen thought she recognized his voice when he said, "Let her go, Julian."

From somewhere behind her she heard low voices. Ellen felt

the pressure from the gun lessen for an instant. Then she gasped as Julian poked her again.

He prodded her toward the foyer. Ellen felt her entire body trembling. There was a good chance that Julian would kill her before the police could stop him.

The light now played on the officer's face. Jeremy King gripped his gun with two hands. "Let her go. Now."

Julian laughed. "Oh, come on now, Jeremy. You've seen enough movies to know better. Do you really think I'm going to release her? Move out of my way so I can get to my desk."

Still aiming the gun at Julian, Jeremy took a step back. "I won't shoot you if you put the gun down, Julian. Drop it, and no one will get hurt."

"No one but me, right? Don't think I've forgotten how you used to bully me."

Jeremy shook his head. "Everyone's all grown up now, Julian. For your own good, put the gun down, and let Ellen go. We'll talk, that's all. This can be worked out. Don't make it any worse."

Julian moved the gun from Ellen's waist to the side of her head. "For Ellen's own good, you drop the gun, or I'll kill her."

Chagrin on the policeman's face ratcheted up Ellen's terror as she watched Jeremy drop his gun. She felt sick with fear, her muscles nearly paralyzed. Julian almost lifted her off her feet as he half dragged her behind the desk. A sob caught in her throat as she realized there was nothing Jeremy could do.

Julian pressed the gun against her temple. "Open the top drawer and take out the set of keys. Don't move anything but your right hand."

Like a puppet, Ellen stood straight, then looked downward. Slowly, she pulled the drawer open, revealing a ring of keys attached to a gold keychain.

Ellen did as she was told, lifting the keys from the drawer. With his left hand, Julian took the keys from her and put them in his pocket. Then with the same hand, he turned Ellen to the right, all the while keeping the gun against her temple with the other. "Move," he told her "We have a long ride ahead of us."

What does that mean? she thought, terrified. *Is he taking me to some remote place where he can commit another murder—mine?*

A second police officer came out of the shadows of the long draperies. His bare hands were held up in surrender. It was Bruce King, with a smile on his face. "There's something you might want to know, Julian. Let's talk."

Julian paused, his left arm tightening around Ellen's waist, his right hand still holding the gun against her head. "What about?"

"You might want to think about the publicity that's going to come out of this. People know you as a man of pride. Surely you don't want this all over the front page of every paper. I say this, because there's a reporter from a Boston paper right here. He's the one who broke in here and called us." Bruce let out a hoarse laugh. "From your own phone. I think you know him. His name is Nick Stanton."

Turning, Ellen saw Nick, being held back by Jeremy King. *It can't be,* Ellen thought *He went back to Boston this morning.*

Nick broke free and started toward Julian.

Bruce lunged for him. "Get down, Stanton!" But Nick was faster, barreling toward Julian.

Julian pulled the gun away from Ellen's head and pointed it wildly at Nick. "You don't belong here," he yelled.

"No!" Ellen screamed as Julian let go of her. A shot sounded across the room. She screamed again as Nick slumped to the floor, blood pouring out from his shoulder. More officers appeared. Someone shouted for her to get down. Ellen crouched under the desk as more shots rang out.

"Don't kill Nick," she pleaded. "Oh, no, please no!"

"Drop the gun, Julian." Jeremy's voice had gone hard.

Ellen heard a lone shot whistle across the room—and knew it had found its target when she heard a thud, like a Halloween pumpkin being smashed on the pavement. A waterfall of blood splashed in front of her and she feared for a moment it was her own.

Julian had fallen hard, behind the desk. His contorted face stared at Ellen in surprise, then blindly. She crawled around his body, straightened up, and ran to Nick. She knelt beside him as an officer loosened Nick's tie and unbuttoned his shirt. The blood from the wound was turning his undershirt a bright red.

"Nick," she whispered, taking his hand. It felt cold, so she brought it to her lips. "Please, oh please, be all right." His eyes opened and he strained to talk.

Bruce knelt beside him. "Be quiet now," he said gently.

"Have to tell her," Nick croaked.

"It can wait," said Ellen, leaning closer.

"No, listen," he said. "Beth is missing. That's why I'm here. Meg called. After the way Julian acted at Beth's birthday party, I thought he had her. My keys ... in the car. Take it."

Nick's hand went limp, and he slumped against Bruce. The faraway whine of a siren came closer. Ellen looked fearfully at the policeman.

"He's lost a lot of blood," Bruce said. "But I don't believe it's life threatening."

"I don't want to leave him," Ellen said, letting the tears fall, "but I have to be with my sister. Her daughter's missing. Will you see that someone looks after him?"

Jeremy nodded to the front door, where three ambulance attendants were rushing in with a stretcher and medical bags. "He'll receive the best care. But the detectives will need to question you."

Ellen kissed Nick's cold cheek. "I'll be back," she said, then ran out the door.

CHAPTER FORTY-FOUR

Thursday, March 17

Meg was lying on her living room couch. A woman about Meg's age sat in a chair beside her. "Who are you?" the woman asked, sounding alarmed when Ellen walked in the door.

"I'm Meg's sister," she said, then stopped, realizing why the woman was staring at her. Her blouse was splattered with blood stains.

"I'll explain later," she promised. "But I need to talk to Meg now."

A washcloth lay across Meg's forehead. She tried to sit up when she saw Ellen. "It's my worst nightmare. Beth is missing."

Taking her sister's hand, which was burning hot, Ellen said, "I know. I'll find her. I will." Meg closed her eyes.

The woman stood. "I'm Lettie, a friend of Meg's. The doctor gave her a sedative, but she's been fighting it. I think it's finally taking hold. Oh, poor, poor dear."

"Thank you for being here, Lettie. But where is Carl? And Matthew?" asked Ellen.

"Carl's out with his brother, looking for a woman who came to this house today. He thinks she may have something to do with it, because Aunt Ruth saw her here earlier and then at the playground where the children were playing. I heard Carl say they were going to the old monastery, the Pomarium. I don't know why."

"Have the police been here?"

"Yes, and I heard the police were also called to the funeral home," Lettie answered. "I don't know what's happening in this town today. But Meg's little boy, Matthew, is all right. He's with Ruth."

"Thank goodness for that," Ellen said, heading toward the staircase. Lettie handed her a sandwich. She hadn't eaten anything since Harvey had given her the toast earlier that day.

Ellen's thoughts swirled around in her head, making her almost dizzy by the time she got upstairs. Theresa knew how to find Meg because she remembered the Anderson house. She had babysat for their boys.

I've got to collect my wits, Ellen thought.

She took a hot shower, changed into the clothes she had worn the day before, and forced herself to eat the sandwich.

After checking on Meg again, she would call the hospital about Nick, then drive Nick's car to Boston, because if her hunch was right, that's where Theresa would be. With Beth.

಄

A police cruiser with flashing blue lights and high-pitched sirens came up behind the Thunderbird and then sped past as Ellen drove into Boston. The distraction gave a moment's respite from her churning thoughts that shook her to the core: her family was very close to being ruined by a man who posed as a friend, one who would commit murder to get his way. She wanted desperately to erase all memory of Julian, especially the image of his lifeless, bloodied body, just inches from her on the floor.

Her thoughts turned to Nick. *I want to be with you. Oh, how I hated leaving you,* she thought. When she had leaned over him as he lay on the floor, wounded, she had smelled his aftershave, the same woodsy fragrance that was still lingering in his car.

Later, when Ellen had called the hospital, she'd been assured that the bullet had been removed and Nick was in recovery. All his vital signs were good. *At least when you wake up, you won't be alone,* she thought. Meg's friends promised to be there for him.

But no one could help Meg. Her daughter was missing. Fear clutched Ellen's heart. She pressed her foot down harder on the accelerator. Meg was in anguish and still feverish. She had to find her niece.

She hoped and prayed her theory was right. Like Carl's Aunt Ruth, Ellen was fairly sure that Theresa was responsible for Beth's disappearance. Ellen was guessing that Theresa acted impulsively. She had somehow gotten the child to go with her and then panicked. But Ellen knew there was at least a chance that Theresa would call her. She didn't have anyone else.

In her apartment, Ellen sat on the edge of her bed and stared at the telephone illuminated by the corner streetlight. It was just past nine p.m. of the longest day of her life. Too tired to get up to put the lights on, she sat, huddled in the dark, willing the phone to ring.

When it did, she grabbed the receiver. "This is Ellen. Don't hang up," she answered quickly.

"I wasn't going to," said Nigel Jackson in his clipped accent. "I wanted you to know that I'm moving on to the sports pages. My assignments with your features department are completed."

Devastated that it wasn't Theresa, Ellen tried to get her mind to switch gears, to focus on her job. "I'm sorry to be losing you," she said, meaning every word. Nigel was one of the finest photographers on any of the city's newspapers.

"Yes, well, I'm sure Marc will find someone else for you. But

there's something you need to know about your feature on homeless women," Nigel went on. "As we suspected, another paper has
put a photographer on the same story. Their guy has been all over
the city, taking shots of what they're calling bag ladies."

Thinking fast, Ellen said, "Here's what we'll do. The photos
you took of the woman and her friend sharing a meal on the
street are powerful enough for a photo feature. We'll go with that
tomorrow and be ahead of the other paper."

"But there's no time to write the captions, Ellen."

"I wrote the captions the day you showed me the photos. I've
got to go. Good luck in the sports department, Nigel." She
wouldn't tell him about Nick, not before Mr. Donovan knew.

"Well, thanks," he said, sounding pleased. "See you around."

The phone rang the minute she hung up. It was Carl, telling
her in a choked voice that the police had searched the Pomarium
and found nothing. He said the police also had led a group of
volunteers through the orchard. Carl's next words made Ellen
shiver. "All they found were dead trees."

CHAPTER FORTY-FIVE

Friday, March 18

Ellen had stayed up half the night, hoping the telephone would ring or the doorbell would buzz. When she had finally gone to bed, the familiar street noises that usually lulled her to sleep had kept her awake.

Now, as she walked to work at six in the morning, she couldn't escape the questions that consumed her: Was it her determination to identify the woman at the cemetery that ultimately caused Beth's disappearance? And was it the same determination to uncover Julian's secrets that landed Nick in the hospital? So *yes*, while she could accept the fact that she had set a lot of this in motion, she couldn't imagine *not* trying to unravel the mysteries that had surrounded her brother. And *yes*, Julian's dangerous obsession with Meg ended before he could hurt anyone else, and a reclusive woman had learned she had a family.

*But Beth was missing—Beth was missing—*the words repeated themselves over and over in Ellen's mind as she stepped into the elevator at work. Nothing mattered except getting Beth back. Her reflection in the glossy walls of the elevator depicted a drawn face with deep shadows beneath her eyes.

When the elevator snapped open on her floor, Ellen found

herself face to face with Marc Donovan. He reached in and pressed the hold button. "You're exhausted," he said. "I want you to go right back to Springton. I'll get you a driver."

"You know what happened?"

"I know about the shoot-out in the funeral home," Marc said wryly. "An old friend of mine is the editor of the Springton weekly paper. Your name came over the police radio, and he remembered your byline from your counterfeiting story. He called me right away."

My last name again, thought Ellen.

"I know you must want to be with your family." Smiling, he added, "And somebody has to take care of Nick."

"I appreciate that," said Ellen. "But there'll be no one in the features department."

"I'm sure Wayne Ellis won't mind filling in," Marc said. "And your pages are in good order."

Ellen thought quickly. Theresa had her business card with her office number on it. She smoothed her hair behind her ear. "That's so nice of you, Mr. Donovan. But I'm better off here, at least for now."

"You know best. Call me if there is anything I can do." He stepped into the elevator that would take him to his office.

When the elevator door slammed shut, Ellen leaned against the wall and took a deep breath, thankful that he hadn't asked more questions. She wondered if she should tell the Boston police about her hunch – that Theresa had taken Beth, and Theresa may get in touch with her. Ellen's gut told her Theresa would never harm Beth, and she hated the idea of the police arresting Theresa. But she also knew that Meg was sick with worry over her daughter. Was there any good solution to this?

She went to her office window and stared down at the pedestrians below, all the while watching for a glimpse of a red scarf.

Her phone rang at eight a.m.

"Yes," Ellen said, her voice filled with tension.

Against a background of traffic noises came a frightened voice. "Ellen? This is Theresa."

"Just tell me you have Beth," said Ellen. Her voice cracking into a whisper, she added, "Please tell me that."

"Yes, I have her. Please believe me, I meant no harm." I only wanted to talk with her at the playground. I asked her if she could go somewhere, anyplace at all, where would it be? And she said, 'Boston, to see the elephants at the circus.'"

"All that matters now is Beth. How is she?"

"She's fine," Theresa said, weariness in her voice. "She's had a wonderful time, but she wants her mother." Her voice catching, Theresa said, "I'm so afraid. I need you to help me get her back."

"Tell me where you are," said Ellen.

"We're across the avenue in a phone booth. Near a newsstand. I can see your building from here."

Ellen stretched the cord as far as it could reach. The steam from a hot pretzel cart rolled across the newsstand, almost blocking it. Ellen remembered there was a public telephone on the corner. It was out of her view.

"Theresa, stay right there."

There was only silence.

"Theresa?" asked Ellen anxiously.

An operator cut in. Another coin was due. Ellen pulled at the cord, as if willing it to bring Theresa back. To her relief, she heard the click of a coin.

"Ellen," Theresa whispered. "Will you promise me one thing?"

"Anything, Theresa. Just bring Beth."

"Please come alone. I'm so ashamed, I can hardly face you."

Ellen had to get to Theresa quickly, and she knew she couldn't risk doing anything that might scare her off.

Out on the avenue, the city had come alive. Ellen waited impatiently for the traffic light to turn red. When it finally did, she elbowed her way through the mass of people crossing the four lanes. Ellen made it as far as the median strip and then stopped when the light, turning green, unleashed a flurry of cars that charged ahead, like race horses released from the starting gate.

Looking across the tops of the speeding vehicles, she saw Theresa stepping out of the phone booth. She clutched her burlap bag which seemed to weigh her down as much as the coat she wore.

Not seeing Beth, Ellen craned her neck to see over the cars and beyond the hoard of pedestrians that blocked her view. She sighed with relief when Theresa came into full view with Beth holding her free hand.

Theresa hesitated, then turned toward the avenue and walked with Beth to the curb. She stood, jostled by the crowd, while Beth, holding a small stuffed animal, appeared to be mesmerized by the traffic.

Impatiently, Ellen stared at the light as if she could will it to change, glancing every few seconds at Theresa and Beth to make sure they weren't swept away in the crowd. Beth's broad smile was a sharp contrast to Theresa, who cast quick, nervous glances in every direction. She had the same look of a trapped animal that Ellen had noticed at the cemetery.

Suddenly, the people around the pair stepped aside, making a clearing so that a man with a camera could get closer. Ellen recognized him as a photographer from her newspaper's competitor. *He must think Theresa is a bag lady*, Ellen realized. He snapped pictures, one after another in rapid succession.

"No! No pictures! Stop!" Ellen screamed, cupping her hands to her mouth. Her words were hopelessly lost in the din of the morning traffic.

He clicked the camera furiously, shooting one frame after another, like a rifleman at target practice.

Theresa looked up, startled, and stepped back. The photographer took advantage of the free space and positioned himself in front of her. She let go of Beth's hand and dropped her bag at the same time and then covered her face with both hands.

Seeing a break in the traffic, Ellen took a step into the avenue but was forced back onto the median by a taxi that appeared to come out of nowhere.

"What, are you crazy, lady?" asked a man behind her.

Seeming to be unaffected by the photographer's actions, Beth waved happily when she spotted Ellen, calling out something. Her words, along with Ellen's command to stay where she was, were lost in the clamor of the traffic.

To Ellen's horror, Beth ran towards her. A scream came from the crowd of pedestrians. A man who looked familiar darted into the traffic behind the little girl, who was already in the second lane.

It was Nigel, on his way to work.

With the agility he was known for, he scooped Beth up by the collar of her coat and narrowly escaped being struck by a car. With Beth's face pressed into his jacket, he stood precariously between the two lanes. Horns blared, brakes screeched. Clutching Beth, Nigel made it safely back across the avenue.

Ellen, who'd felt as if her heart had stopped, now breathed easier as Nigel set Beth down on the sidewalk. The traffic that had halted started up again. Ellen waited for the light to turn so she could make her way over to Nigel and her niece. Beth, looking no worse for her adventure, was still in Nigel's arms.

And then Ellen saw something that made her blood freeze. Almost as if she didn't see the traffic, Theresa wandered into the busy avenue, heading straight for the median where Ellen stood.

"Go back, Theresa," Ellen pleaded. "For God's sake, go back."

Theresa headed to Ellen, her hands outstretched. "Ask them to forgive me," she said.

"Don't come any farther!" Ellen screamed.

Smiling, Theresa stepped in front of an oncoming truck. Ellen squeezed her eyes shut at the sound of the squealing brakes. She opened them after she heard a deafening thump.

Theresa lay in a crumpled heap, a ribbon of blood streaking alongside the red scarf around her neck.

Traffic lanes had come to a complete stop. The screams of the pedestrians drowned out the noise of the idling vehicles.

Ellen ran into the middle of the avenue and knelt beside Theresa. "I'm here." she whispered. Tenderly, she stroked Theresa's forehead. Warm blood trickled through her fingers. "Theresa, please believe me, I came here alone as I said I would. Oh, I'm so sorry," she sobbed.

Theresa's eyes fluttered and then opened wide. Taking quick, short breaths, she spoke in a barely audible whisper. "Nothing's your fault. Thank you for helping me find the family I never knew I had. They are so beautiful. I am so thankful to you."

The wail of sirens came closer. A police car made its way through the halted traffic. An officer ordered spectators to keep moving. Cars honked, people hurried by, business as usual as a city resumed its daily routine right around them.

"You better move, too, lady," said the officer, now standing beside her. "The ambulance is on its way."

"I want to hear what she is saying," insisted Ellen, bending over Theresa, whose eyes were closed. Her face looked serene and angelic. Blood continued to stream down the side of her face. She mumbled incoherently.

"It's a shame," said the officer, "that more can't be done to help somebody like this."

"This somebody," said Ellen, "is one of my family." She lowered her head, this time sideways so her ear was just above Theresa's lips. She covered her other ear to block out the traffic noise and the policeman's whistle.

"What are you saying, Theresa?" she pleaded. Theresa had lapsed into Latin. "*Sed non culpa mea est*. But the blame is not mine."

An ambulance careened to a stop behind the police car. A medic rushed over, carrying a medical bag. He leaned down, placed his fingers on Theresa's neck, and then looked up at Ellen, about to say something.

"You don't have to tell me," Ellen said. "I know she's left us."

CHAPTER FORTY-SIX

Tuesday, March 19

Springton, Massachusetts

The sounds of footsteps woke her. Ellen strained to sit up but the pain in her joints put her back down. She'd been asleep all day in Meg's spare room.

Meg opened the door and set a tray down, then took Ellen's temperature. When she took the thermometer out of Ellen's mouth, she held it to the light. "It's down a bit," Meg said. "Just under a hundred."

"I can't believe I came down with the flu," Ellen said. "Everything is such a blur. I remember the police drove me and Beth to Springton on Friday and later I visited Nick at the Hospital."

Meg put her finger to her lips. "Don't do any more talking," she said. "You just need to know that Nick was discharged this morning. He's already in Boston and is determined to be back at work tomorrow."

Ellen grabbed Meg's arm. "Am I delirious or did Nick ask me to marry him when I saw him at the hospital? And did I really say yes?"

Meg laughed. "Yes, you're going to be Mrs. Nicholas Stanton very soon. And you also said that I could handle the wedding arrangements."

Ellen shook her head. Had she agreed to that? She couldn't imagine discussing wedding arrangements now. Just the idea of getting out of bed seemed exhausting.

Smoothing down the bed covers, Meg said, "You probably caught the flu from me. But I don't think your standing out in the cold for Theresa's funeral yesterday helped any."

Ellen closed her eyes and thought about the funeral.

A small group of mourners had attended Theresa's afternoon graveside service at the Von Der Hyde plot. After the service, the small car procession had passed by "Rose Garden," an area in the cemetery with a pyramid-shaped monument emblazoned with the Baker name. Wendell, the driver of the car in which Meg and Ellen were riding, had pointed to it, saying, "The likes of that Julian shouldn't be allowed in this cemetery. Nobody but me was at his funeral this morning, and that's just because I was paid to drive the hearse."

Ellen didn't want to think about Julian. She opened her eyes and concentrated on Meg, who put a cup of tea in Ellen's hands and then reached for a cup for herself. "Talk about things going around again," said Meg.

Ellen made a face; the tea was bitter. "What do you mean?"

"I'm thinking of the day four years ago when we all came back here after Mom and Dad's funerals. I've never thought about it but now I understand."

Ellen tried to fight off the sleep that weighed on her. For days, Meg had refused to discuss anything. Now Ellen was not about to lose the chance. "Talk to me, Meg. Please tell me what happened that day."

Meg removed some tea leaves with a dainty spoon. "After their funerals, I was on the verge of collapse. I was pregnant with Beth. I came up here to lie down, and Eric came in a few minutes later.

"He sat right where I'm sitting now, on this bed. I was very self-conscious at first. After all, he was practically a stranger to me. He sat for the longest time, and I remember a kind of peaceful feeling, maybe a connection to Mom and Dad. But now I know it was more than that."

"What did he say?"

Meg sighed and put down her tea cup. "He took my hands in both of his, and oh, Ellen, they were so large and strong. He examined my hands on both sides and stroked my fingers. He whispered something like, 'They're just like hers.' Then he held them to his face. It's possible that he thought I was asleep."

"Did he tell you anything about himself or Theresa?"

"No," Meg said. "It's as if ... well, like he just wanted to be with me. I guess he decided to leave things as they were."

"I don't blame him. Think of the consequences."

"No matter what, the parents I knew will always be my mom and dad, in my heart and forever. Still, I wish I'd gotten the chance to really know Eric."

"Me, too," Ellen said.

Meg shuddered. "That woman, Theresa. I hate that she took Beth."

"You have every right to feel that way," Ellen said quietly. "But think of the shock it must have been for a mother to find out that the baby she thought was dead for twenty-five years was all the time growing up just a short distance away."

In a firm voice, Meg said, "I know I'll be able to feel some sympathy for her sometime in the future but it's all too much for me right now." She stood and picked up the tray. "Harvey tells me that with Theresa dead, I'll inherit Chief Lake's house." Meg paused at the door. "I told him I don't want it. Harvey recommends selling it and investing the money for the children's education. I've asked him to handle the sale, and even though he doesn't want payment, I'll insist on paying him a generous commission." Meg smiled. "Then he can get his house repaired, and I'll remind him of his favorite words."

"Let me guess," said Ellen. "Everything that goes around, comes around." She closed her eyes and had the best sleep she'd had in a very long time.

CHAPTER FORTY-SEVEN

Saturday, May 7, 1955

Springton, Massachusetts

Her arm looped through Harvey's, Ellen walked slowly between the short aisle of folding chairs arranged in Meg's living room. In the back of the room, Meg's friend Lettie played the piano, the only possession Meg allowed herself to keep from Chief Lake's house. She had told Ellen she couldn't explain why she wanted it, but maybe she could learn to play one day.

Ellen could hardly stop herself from running to Nick, who was so handsome in his light gray three-piece suit, standing beside the fireplace, which was festooned with sprigs of lilacs and yards of white ribbon. Carl stood with Matthew, who held a pillow with the wedding rings. They were smiling as broadly as the groom.

Ellen's smile was as natural as the afternoon sunlight filtering through the windows. She was happy that Meg had convinced her to keep most of the traditions, even though it was a small wedding. And she had to admit that Meg's choice of her wedding gown—a tea-length, A-line dress in a cream color with embroidered organdy trim and a bow belt—was perfect. She saw the admiration in Nick's eyes.

Harvey, steadying himself with his cane, put Ellen's hand in Nick's. Ellen gave her bouquet of lilacs to Beth, who, when she smiled, revealed star-shaped dimples. Meg, glowing in a pearl-pink dress, hugged Ellen.

Stefan Nowak, with his parents and grandmother smiling proudly from their seats, gave the scripture reading.

Nick and Ellen faced Reverend Martin. The piano became quiet. *We've had funerals and now a wedding,* Ellen thought. *There's been enough sorrow and pain. Today is a day for joy.*

After the wedding vows, the minister pronounced Nick and Ellen man and wife. While the thirty-six guests applauded, Nick and Ellen kissed and then turned to walk up the aisle. The pianist resumed playing. From the porch, Harvey's dog, Piper, howled along with his own high notes, much to the delight of Matthew and Beth, who loved him as much as they loved his owner.

Nick whispered in Ellen's ear. "I say no wedding is complete without a singing dog. This is a wonderful surprise, don't you think, Mrs. Stanton?"

"Oh, this is only the beginning, Nick Stanton," murmured Ellen. "I have a feeling our lives are going to be filled with surprises."

EPILOGUE

On the morning of the Fourth of July, Meg and Ellen sat on a swing on Meg's front porch, sipping lemonade. Carl and Nick had left earlier to take Beth and Matthew to the parade in town. Meg put down her glass and unfolded a letter that Officer Jeremy King had given her. A letter he had found in Julian's desk.

"Are you sure you're ready to read Eric's letter?" Ellen asked softly, setting down her glass and putting her arm around Meg. "Do you need more time?"

"Four months has been long enough," Meg said emphatically. "Even though I learned what Eric wanted me to know, in a way he never would have intended... I'm ready to read his own words... in this letter that Julian stole from us."

Together, Meg and Ellen read the letter.

My Dear Meg,

If you are reading this, it means my illness traveled so fast that it destroyed my ability to talk with you. These words are meant to be said, not written, and I'm so sorry things have to be this way. Meg, twenty-five years ago, a beautiful young lady gave birth to a beautiful baby girl, and she is you. You are my daughter. I was not aware that I had fathered a child until my parents died four years ago, when circumstances led me to the discovery that Esther and Rudolph Von Der Hyde brought you up as their own child. I only wish they were here so I could thank them with all my heart and soul. Please accept, for reasons you may not understand, that it is best that your biological mother not be identified, though it is possible that her name will be known to you one day. Please trust me on this. I ask you to stay close to Ellen and tell her she was the best kid sister in the world. I love you all. Please forgive me.

Your father, Eric Von Der Hyde

The two sisters were silent for a while, then Ellen asked, "What do you think?"

Meg shrugged. "It's exactly what you uncovered. He wanted me to know the truth, that he was my actual father."

Ellen nodded. "And yet, he protected Theresa. He wasn't going to give her identity away until she was ready to be known. I think all our questions have been answered. The only thing Eric didn't know was that over the years Julian changed from being a friend to a betrayer."

"Please," Meg said. "I'm not ready to talk about Julian." She hesitated, then said, "Except that ... I still wish you and Nick would take some of the money. Really, after the horrible things he did ... you could buy a house with it."

"Nick and I will earn our own money to buy a house," Ellen said firmly. "I'm not taking a cent that came from Julian." She hadn't asked Meg how she had felt when she learned that she had not only inherited Chief Lake's and Eric's estates, but was the sole beneficiary of Julian's estate.

Meg sipped the last of her iced tea and set the glass on a table next to her chair. "Did you hear about the auction?"

Ellen shook her head. "You told me the funeral home and its contents were going up for sale. But you never mentioned anything about an auction."

Meg gave a long sigh. "Well, I'll get to that in a minute. Fortunately, the sale of the funeral home is no problem. The owners of Cedar's Funeral Home are buying the building and everything in it. At my request, the King brothers cleared out all those horrid photos of me and burned them. That's how they found the letter I just read to you. The one that Julian stole."

Meg shuddered and said, "Now about the auction. I heard that Julian's portrait of me wound up at an art auction in Boston."

"Art?" Ellen echoed, unable to believe anyone would want an object she had found so repulsive. Much less, consider it art.

"It sold for six figures," Meg said quietly.

"To whom?" Ellen demanded.

Meg shrugged. "I don't know. The buyer remained anonymous."

"That's almost as disturbing as the painting itself," Ellen said.

"All I care about is that we never have to see it again," Meg declared. "Julian is out of our lives now. We can just forget all about him."

Ellen knew she'd never be able to forget that horrific day in the funeral home, but she made herself smile and said, "I'll do my best."

Meg leaned over and put her arm around Ellen. "The only good thing about this whole mess is that you and I became so much closer. Promise me you'll keep visiting Springton, and we won't lose each other again."

"I promise," said Ellen, and she hugged her back.

THE END

ABOUT THE AUTHOR

Secrets of the Orchard is Jean Kelly's first novel, one of many "rainy day" writing projects she began after her three children were grown. Jean is a lifelong Rhode Islander and a graduate of the University of Rhode Island with a BA degree in English. She is a short story writer and has a background in newspaper writing and public relations. Visit Jean at www.jean-kelly.com

Made in the USA
Middletown, DE
08 May 2020

93751364R00146